FAMILY MEN

FAMILY MEN

STORIES BY
STEVE YARBROUGH

Louisiana State University Press   Baton Rouge and London   1990

Copyright © 1984, 1986, 1987, 1988, 1989, 1990 by Steve Yarbrough
All rights reserved
Manufactured in the United States of America
First printing
99 98 97 96 95 94 93 92 91 90   5 4 3 2 1

Designer: *Amanda McDonald Key*
Typeface: *Century Old Style*
Typesetter: *G &S Typesetters, Inc.*
Printer and binder: *Thomson-Shore, Inc.*

Library of Congress Cataloging-in-Publication Data

Yarbrough, Steve, date.
    Family men : stories / by Steve Yarbrough.
      p. cm.
    ISBN 0-8071-1619-X (alk. paper)
    I. Title.
    PS3575.A717F36   1990
    813'.54—dc20   90-32793
                               CIP

The author offers grateful acknowledgment to the editors of the following pub-
lications, in which stories in this book originally appeared: *Cimarron Review* (October, 1987), "A Green Card" (originally entitled "Maryla"); *Crazyhorse* (Fall,
1986), "The Right Kind of Person"; *Kansas Quarterly* (November, 1986), "The
Lode Sentry"; *Literary Review* (Summer, 1988), "Sara"; *Missouri Review* (Fall,
1986), "Some Glad Morning"; *Passages North* (Summer, 1988), "The Trip";
South Dakota Review (Summer, 1988), "The Full Ride"; *Southern Review* (Summer, 1984), "Family Men"; *Virginia Quarterly Review* (Winter, 1988), "Between
Now and Then."

"Born Again" first appeared in *The Hudson Review.*

Publication of this book has been supported by a grant from the National
Endowment for the Arts in Washington, D.C., a federal agency.

The paper in this book meets the guidelines for permanence and durability of the
Committee on Production Guidelines for Book Longevity of the Council on Library Resources. ∞

For Ewa, my Polish love

CONTENTS

THE RIGHT KIND OF PERSON   1

THREE CHEERS FOR ELLIS FULLER   15

SARA   28

THE LODE SENTRY   47

BORN AGAIN   60

FAMILY MEN   76

BETWEEN NOW AND THEN   85

THE TRIP   104

A GREEN CARD   116

THE FULL RIDE   134

SOME GLAD MORNING   149

THE RIGHT KIND OF PERSON

ANN had just bent over to put on her shoes when she began to feel as if her head was full of fog. For the longest time her mind stayed cloudy. When she finally had a thought, it was, *All my life thinking's been easy and now it's hard.* She bet she'd had a darned stroke.

"Momma?"

She stared at the mirror over her dresser. She didn't look the least bit different. Her hair was still more red than grey, her teeth were still white.

"Better hurry, Momma, or we'll both be late."

Her daughter Darlene stood at the door.

Maybe the stroke was just a little one—else she wouldn't have recognized her daughter, would she? When her sister Lena had the stroke two years ago, she didn't even know her own husband. Ann bent and put on her shoes easy as eating an egg.

She was waiting in the car when Darlene opened the door. "I hope it don't sleet," Darlene said. "The weatherman's saying sleet and snow and I don't know what all. Johnny says every time Billy sends him to Jackson the weather turns awful."

All the way downtown Darlene ran her mouth. Stroke or no stroke, Ann did what she always did. She tuned out to avoid

thinking ill of her daughter. Darlene was like her daddy had
been. She talked all the time because she was afraid that if she
shut up, even for a minute, you might tell her something she
didn't want to hear.

Darlene stopped the car in front of Kenwin's. Ann opened her
door and climbed out.

"Bye, Momma."

Ann said, "Bye."

Or tried to: nothing came out. Her bowels loosened a little
when she realized she was standing in the middle of the street,
in downtown Indianola, with her mouth hanging open. She shut it
quick. "Mmm," she mumbled. She smiled at Darlene—to keep
her from having a heart attack in the unlikely event that she'd
noticed anything unusual—then she slammed the car door and
went in to work.

All day long she refused to open her mouth. She just smiled
when someone spoke to her. A couple of customers looked at
her funny, but thank the Lord she had sense enough to show
them whatever they wanted; she could still tell a skirt from a pair
of panty hose. Thank the Lord too that this was Christmas rush.
The place was so busy Velma Boyle couldn't come yapping.

When they closed at five, Velma said, "Ann, are you feeling
normal? You've been awful quiet."

Ann grinned and waved good-bye.

Darlene talked all the way home, but this time Ann felt glad.
She'd slipped into the bathroom around three-thirty and tried to
say, "Good day." She had "Good day" in her mind, she knew
how it ought to sound, but her mouth couldn't seem to form the
words. She'd decided the stroke was probably worse than she'd
first thought, but she still believed she could lick it if they'd just
leave her be. She was happy Johnny Garber had gone to Jackson. If the weather got bad and iced the roads, she might have
time to bring herself around before he returned. Her sister had

died in a Rolling Fork rest home last summer. Ann didn't want to give her son-in-law the chance to pack her off to Care Inn.

At supper Darlene found her out. She asked her two or three questions about did she want this or would she like that, and Ann couldn't muster an answer. She might have solved that problem simply by filling her plate and then shoveling food into her mouth, but her right hand had gone numb and she knew she couldn't handle a fork. She sat still and quiet, the hand asleep in her lap.

"Momma." Darlene's eyes were getting bigger. "Momma, what's wrong?"

Her voice cracked on "wrong." Ann wanted to say, "Don't commence, Darlene."

Darlene shoved food at her crying, "This! Can you say what this is? Or this?"

Johnny got home before too long, and Ann guessed it was a good thing. Darlene was about ready to roll on the floor; she'd done that the night her daddy died, though she was nearly fifty at the time.

Johnny Garber stood over Ann. She wished she could get up from the table, but her right leg felt funny. If only she hadn't sat down. She should have known better.

"Ann," Johnny said. "Are you sick?"

She looked up at him and shook her head no. Then she did something she'd almost never done. She smiled at her son-in-law.

"We better call the hospital," he said.

Darlene cried, "Oh, Jesus!"

Ann shook her head no, no, please no, but Johnny was already dialing.

·   ·   ·

"Stay in the car," Johnny said. "I'll come around and help you out."

She waited until he slammed the door; then, using her left

hand, she opened her own door. She heaved both her legs out of the car and somehow managed to stand. Back at the house, when she realized Johnny intended to tote her, she'd willed herself to walk. Now she aimed to do it again.

Cold rain pelted her face. "Goddam it," Johnny said. He held his umbrella over her head and tried to steady her with his arm, but she shook him off like an unpleasant dream. She walked around the car and up the wheelchair ramp to the building. She tried her best to hurry because the highway was only a few feet away and she didn't want anybody to drive by and see her.

A nurse was waiting for them. "Come right in here, darling," she said. She led them into an examining room filled almost entirely by a leather-covered table with white paper rolled over it. "Let's have you lie down."

While the nurse strapped the blood-pressure contraption onto her arm, she asked Johnny how Ann had been behaving.

"She won't say anything."

"Is she normally very talkative?"

"She usually expresses her opinions."

The nurse took her blood pressure, wrote it on a clipboard, and said Dr. North would be there in a few minutes.

Johnny had left Darlene behind to collect insurance papers. She and North appeared at the same time. North looked at the nurse's clipboard, shined a light in Ann's eyes, listened to her chest, and told her she'd had a mild stroke.

Upon hearing the word "stroke," Darlene squealed and slid to the floor.

While her daughter occupied Johnny's and North's attention, Ann hopped off the table. But something went wrong, her legs had turned to cheese, and the next thing she knew, she was on the floor too, scant inches away from Darlene.

•   •   •

Ann had moved in with her daughter and son-in-law three years ago when Early died. She'd moved because Johnny begged her. "You can't live out there in the country by yourself," he said. "What in the world would you do?"

"I'd do what I've always done."

"What if you get down sick?"

"If I get down sick, I'll get up well."

"Somebody might bust in on you."

"They do, I'll blow them halfway to Jackson. I got a shotgun for just such as that."

"Well, then," he said, "you ought to move in with us for Darlene's sake. She'll worry."

It hadn't occurred to her that this might happen. She'd always figured that if Early went before she did, she'd stay on her farm and work till she died. But now, she saw, Johnny was fixing to beg her to come live with him—else Darlene would keep him awake every night for the rest of his life—and while she didn't want to live with Johnny any more than he wanted her to, she truly loved this whole minute; she wished she could preserve it, seal it in a jar.

"Ann," he said, looking down at his toes, "please let me move you. Don't make me beg too long."

"There's certain conditions I'll want met."

His blue gaze grew wary. "What kind of conditions?"

"I'll apprise you of them," she said, "as they come to me."

The morning after he moved her, she rose early, lugged her orange trunk with the leather handle into the living room, and took out her pictures. The pictures of Grandpa Michalson in his coffin, she decided, would look nice hanging over the TV. She pawed through the trunk until she found her hammer and nails.

Johnny's walls were white Sheetrock, smooth and unmarked. She positioned a nail.

The loudness of the first blow thrilled her. She began to beat the hell out of the wall. A second nail was halfway in when she sensed an unhappy presence. She glanced over her shoulder. Sleepy-eyed Johnny wore a pair of blue shorts. "Morning," she said. "Remember them conditions I mentioned?" She hit the wall another blow. "I thought of what one of them is. I have to have my pictures. They'll make me feel at home. If she sees I feel at home, Darlene won't worry about me so much, and if Darlene don't worry—"

Johnny turned and trudged away.

Later that same morning, at breakfast, she forgot and read the paper aloud; she'd been doing that for years, because if she didn't Early would jabber on and on about his ingrown toenail or Hiram Knight's new John Deere, and she didn't want to hear that; but she'd made up her mind not to read aloud at Johnny's, because she didn't want to plant the notion she was senile.

She'd just gotten through the part about how the child-murderer down in Crystal Springs buried the body of his own three-year-old in a grave on the banks of the Pearl River, when Johnny threw down his fork, stood up, and stomped out of the room.

"He feels like life's full of bad news," Darlene told her the next day. She was explaining it in such an orderly fashion that Ann knew Johnny must have written it down for her. "You know, he's never been too happy with his job, and Billy didn't give him a raise for next year. Most everybody else at the plant got one. He says we'll make it, but just barely.

"He says with things being bad in general, it just upsets him to hear about disaster and killing when he's trying to eat."

"Things *are* bad in general," Ann said. "But if Johnny was the right kind of person, he'd fall down on his knees and thank God they're not worse."

That evening, as Johnny sat slumped on the couch, a six-pack at his side, Ann said, "Tomorrow I'm going out and hunt me a job." She'd planned on finding a job anyway, even though she knew Johnny wouldn't like it; now he'd given her an excuse. "Between your little salary and Darlene's and mine, we'll make it just fine, don't you worry."

"Shit." He slammed his beer can down on the coffee table. "You're seventy-three years old. Job, my ass."

"I start work in the morning," she said at supper the next night.

Johnny's fork halted halfway to his mouth.

"The weatherman," Darlene babbled, "he says it might rain. Or it might not. There's only a fifty percent—"

"Shut up, Darlene," Ann and Johnny said together.

Darlene did. Blessed silence.

"I don't know who'd be fool enough to hire a woman your age," Johnny finally said, "but whoever it is, you can just call them up and tell them thanks but no thanks."

"When the Lord gets ready for a person to lay down and quit," Ann told him, "they'll know it. Quit'll be all they *can* do. Till then, everybody ought to strive. I'm gonna be a salesgirl at Kenwin's."

Johnny laid his fork down and stood up. "Ann," he said, "you're impossible. God help you."

"God won't help me," she said, "if I don't help myself. You've got to be willing to meet Him halfway."

•   •   •

Every time Johnny rose from his chair that first night, the cushion sighed. She'd hear his soles clop twice, then she'd feel him standing over her.

And she'd wonder what he saw when he saw her. She remembered the way her sister looked the last time she saw her at the rest home: a pale green bib tucked under her chin, applesauce oozing from the corner of her mouth as a teenaged nurse spoon-fed her. She'd be damned if she aimed to be spoon-fed.

The next morning North pried her eyes open and shined his

infernal light in each one. He listened to her heart, he glanced at his clipboard, then he told her she was doing just fine.

"Would you be doing fine," she wished she could ask, "if you couldn't raise up and say, 'Scat'?"

"And," North went on, "your daughter's fine too. She'll be in to see you in a few minutes."

He left without saying a word about sending her home.

Johnny came to stand by the bed. She stole a peek at him to see if he looked like he pitied her. If he did, he was masking it well. He looked like regular Johnny. "You want to watch the television?" he asked her.

She shook her head no.

"How about the paper? Want to read the paper?"

She didn't care what was happening to anybody but her, and the paper couldn't tell her a thing about that. She shook her head again and closed her eyes.

Darlene flittered in. She poked her face right down in Ann's. "We took us a tumble last night! Wonder we didn't bust something!" she chirped. "I'm going to stay with you and let Johnny go home and take a bath."

As soon as Johnny had closed the door, the TV blared on. "Let's us watch 'The Guiding Light,'" Darlene said. "Won't that be a good way to spend the time?"

"Yes, Darlene," Ann longed to say, "that's every bit as good a way to spend the time as twiddling your thumbs or picking your nose."

She guessed having her daughter for a wife must be every bit as trying as having had Early for a husband. She wondered where she and Johnny Garber went wrong.

•   •   •

She had lived with her son-in-law before.

When Johnny left the Navy in the fall of '46, he came back to

Mississippi and began dating Darlene. He was the first boy she'd ever gone out with, so Ann was surprised that winter when Darlene said she wanted to get married.

Her inclination was to say no, because Darlene was just sixteen, but Johnny's daddy, Mr. Lee Roy Garber, came to her and said, "Ann, Darlene's the most harmless girl in the world, and I don't want you to worry about Johnny being good to her, because if he's not I'll kill him."

They got married in March. Mr. Garber fixed them up a house on his place, and he bought them an old school bus, which he and Johnny equipped with an ice-cream freezer and a soft-drink box and a couple of candy counters. For a good three years Johnny and Darlene supported themselves by driving the rolling store around the countryside and selling stuff to hoe hands and tractor drivers.

Then Mr. Garber passed away. By this time Ann had seen enough of Johnny to know why his daddy had made a merchant of him instead of a farmer. Johnny was lazy. For the past two or three months he'd operated the rolling store alone—Darlene was working in town at Morgan & Lindsey's—and a couple of times, as she hauled a load of cotton to the gin, Ann had come upon the school bus parked beneath a shade tree by the side of the road. Through the window she glimpsed Johnny on the candy counter napping.

When Mr. Garber died, his wife sold the farm and moved to Arizona to live with her sister. The man who bought the farm said Johnny and Darlene could keep living there, but of course they'd have to pay rent.

"Mark my words," Ann told Early. "They'll have to move out. Johnny's not making any money. If I was Darlene's daddy, I'd whip his tail. A man's supposed to provide for his wife."

Early said, "Time to slop the hogs," and went outside.

Darlene came to ask if she and Johnny could move in with her parents. Ann could tell she was embarrassed; she kept her big eyes trained on the floor. "It'll just be for a little while," she said. "Johnny says he's thinking about buying us a house in Belzoni."

"Why Belzoni?"

"He says Belzoni's a nicer town than Indianola."

"What makes it nicer?"

"Well . . . they've got the livestock auctions there."

"Does Johnny aim to ranch cattle?"

Darlene said she didn't think so.

"Then why would the auction being there make it nicer?"

Darlene ran her tongue over her lower lip. Her face brightened. "The Yazoo River runs near there."

"Oh, honey," Ann said. "You've married a trifling man."

Darlene erupted. While she cried, Ann held her and smoothed her blowzy hair. "You know you can come here," she said. "What's mine's yours."

They moved in the next weekend. Ann gave them the big room at the back of the house; she'd always loved that room because when the wind blew, the branches of the big old cedar tree that stood nearby made music; and sometimes, when Indian Bayou flooded, you could hear water lapping tree bark. Of course, she guessed if it ever flooded bad enough, the water might get in the house. It amused her to imagine Johnny Garber trying to paddle out in a boat. *Between him and Early,* she thought, *we'd doubtless spill and drown.*

One afternoon, after he'd been living there a month or so, Johnny came home about three o'clock. Ann was sitting on the couch shelling peas. When Johnny walked in, she said, "Did you sell much?"

"Not too much."

She glanced up at him. He was a nice-looking young man, tall like all the men in his family, slim-hipped, jut-jawed, and he had a pair of powder-blue eyes.

"If you didn't sell much," she said, "maybe you ought to get back out and beat the bushes."

He stood before the mantelpiece, studying the pictures on it. "Ann," he said, "what is it about dead people that appeals to you?"

"What?"

"You've got nine pictures up here," he said, "and four of them are shots of people in their coffins. You've even got two pictures of the same corpse taken from different angles."

"That's my grandpa. Grandpa Michalson."

"That *was* your grandpa. In these pictures he's something else altogether."

"I don't have no pictures of him living," she said. "You're cold-hearted, Johnny, if you can't love your dead."

"When somebody's dead there's nothing to love. I respect a corpse enough not to hop around popping pictures of it."

"If you don't like my pictures," she said, "you can always move into the bus. You already spend a lot of time sleeping in it."

He faced her. "Did you know I sleep there most nights?" he said. "There's just one bed in our room. My presence might make your daughter uncomfortable." He walked out before she could reply, which was probably a good thing, because she didn't know what to say.

The next day, he didn't speak to her or Early. She did her best to act nice. At mealtime she asked him did he want some blackeyes or some turnips, but he just sat there, not making a sound. He parked his chair at an angle to the table, so that Ann saw only his back. And the day after that, while she was chopping cotton in the field across the road from the house, she saw a pickup truck turn into her yard and let a man out. The pickup pulled away, and the man stood in the yard conversing with Johnny. Soon, Johnny and the man shook hands. The man climbed into the bus, cranked it, and drove off.

She dug her hoe into the soft dirt on top of her row and left it standing there to mark her spot. When she got to the house, Johnny was lying on the couch reading. She pulled the book out of his hand.

She looked at the cover. "*The Sea-Wolf,*" she said. "Twenty-four years old and laying up reading animal stories." She handed the book back. "Who was that in the bus?"

"Raymond Ferris."

"From the tractor company?"

"Yeah."

"What's he doing with the bus?"

"He bought it."

"Bought it?"

"Yeah. Or anyway he's buying it. He don't have the money yet."

"How do you plan to make a living from now on?"

"Darlene's working."

Ann's heart began to pound. "I know she's working," she said. "She's working, Early's working, I'm working—and you're too lazy to drive that damn bus down the road and sell Popsicles to niggers. How much energy can it take to sell a nigger a Popsicle?"

"More than I've got," Johnny said and reopened his book.

She was amazed. "So you don't aim to do any work for the rest of your life?"

"What reason have I got to work?"

"Reason?" she said.

"When you work you're supposed to be working toward something. I don't see no end in sight."

"I work," Ann said, "because a person's supposed to earn their living by sweat of their brow."

Johnny swung his legs off the couch. "I'll tell you why you work from daylight till dark," he said. "You do it to forget you're married to a man who don't have stomach enough to shoot a stray dog. You do it because it keeps you too busy to wonder how you'll make it through the day when you can't do it no more."

She waited until she was sure her voice would sound calm. "Johnny," she said, "I want you out of my house by tomorrow night. With no roof over your head and no grub in your gut, you'll have ample reason to toil."

•   •   •

Christmas passed. She stayed in the hospital day after day, feeling worse and worse. For one thing, she still couldn't talk; yet once a day a nurse brought by a poster board on which had been glued drawings of a piece of pie, an apple, a glass of milk, all sorts of foods and drinks. "Can you remember the word for this?" the nurse would ask, pointing at a greenish-looking hamburger. When she didn't answer, the nurse would withdraw the poster, promising, "You'll tell us tomorrow."

She couldn't walk anymore either. Every time she tried, her right leg gave way. Once, when Johnny was helping her to the bathroom, her left leg went rubbery too. When she fell, Johnny caught her. She heard a raspy "goddam" and for an instant felt almost gleeful—she'd said something—but then she realized it was Johnny's "goddam" and not hers. She would've said it if she could.

She quit eating because nothing tasted right and also because she couldn't control the muscles in her mouth; food oozed down her chin, and Darlene wiped it off, cooing, "It's just a little mess is all." When she refused to eat, they stuck a needle in her arm and fed her through a tube. They catheterized her and laid a plastic bag on the bed.

She no longer felt responsible for keeping herself alive. It was someone else's doing.

Looking at Johnny Garber, tired and greying in his chair, she thought, *This is where you was when you was laying on my couch. I made you get up and turn a hand.*

•   •   •

"Here we go, Mrs. King," the nurse said.

Ann barely knew who she was. She let Johnny and the nurse lift her into the wheelchair. The day before, she'd heard North tell Johnny that as soon as she got stronger, she'd have to go to the Rehabilitation Center in Jackson. He said they might be able to help her regain the use of her arm and leg; they might even teach her to talk. Her sister had gone to the Rehab Center after her stroke; then it was on to the rest home in Rolling Fork.

They rolled her out to the parking lot, talking to her all the way, but she paid them no mind. She closed her eyes.

When she opened them, she was sitting in Johnny's driveway. Darlene stared at her with red streaks in her eyes.

Johnny got out of the car, then opened Ann's door. She let him lift her in his arms.

She saw the strain on his face as he toted her across the yard. *You're not a young man anymore, Johnny Garber,* she thought. *And me, I'm an old, feeble woman.*

He carried her not to her bedroom but to the living-room couch. "You need to make a daily habit of sitting up," he said, "even if it's just for a few minutes."

Ann felt weaker than most folks' faith, and she knew she'd hoed her last row. But she sat there half an hour, looking out the window, and watched some neighbor boys shoot baskets in the yard across the street.

THREE CHEERS FOR
ELLIS FULLER

O VER the years Lucille Mitchell had been the victim of numerous pranks. Every Halloween the kids made her yard look like a Charmin warehouse that a hurricane had hit. Often, when she left school in the afternoon, she'd find all four tires flat, which meant she'd have to take the hand pump from her trunk and stand there pumping and heaving to get them reinflated. Many an eggshell had cracked against her front door, and her eardrums had suffered a barrage of shrieks and whistles when she answered her phone.

She graded toughly, brooked no dalliance in the classroom, and while she doubted that many of her students actually hated her, she knew that none of them liked her. Worse yet, she couldn't tell that her teaching had the slightest effect. Most students made the same grades at the end of a term that they'd made at the beginning; a few got worse. After a while she lost heart. When she'd accumulated thirty years' service in the Indianola school system, she decided to retire.

Immediately the pranks stopped. She was grateful for that, but soon she had other problems. She did not know how to spend her time. She had no husband, no kids, no very close friends, just one sister who lived all the way out in California. She'd never been one to go to church, and she'd never read much of anything except eighth-grade science texts and related teaching materials. She liked movies, but the Indianola Theatre had closed during the sixties, and she thought it was silly to drive to Greenville every evening just to see a show. Mostly she watched TV and messed around in her garden and expanded her already-wide waistline with snacks and desserts. She'd lost control of her appetite many years ago, and her only remnant of self-restraint was her refusal to let anyone see her overeating.

She'd just finished off a big lunch, with a bowl of Breyers for dessert, when the letter came. It was in a business envelope with no return address. She opened it on her way to the garden.

Dear Ms. Mitchell,

I have waited many years to write this letter. I feared you might have me arrested. I *still* fear you might have me arrested, but I no longer fear being arrested. I've concluded that jails are as various in kind as the species and genera you used to teach us about. A jail of the type the police would put me in might represent an improvement in my living conditions. But that's my problem and not yours.

I have for quite some time felt a strong affinity for you both in an emotional and physical sense. I propose we meet for a date. I don't know what people do on dates, so if you do you'll have to tell me, and if you don't we'll contrive to find out.

Obviously, I want to spare us both embarrassment. If you're uninterested, frightened, or repelled by my suggestion, don't answer your phone when it rings next Tuesday evening between 6:00 and 6:15. If you are even slightly interested, take the phone off the hook so that I'll get a busy signal. If that happens, I'll contact you within three days by mail.

She carried the letter inside, made herself a cup of coffee, and sat down on the couch to examine the envelope. It bore a Vicksburg postmark. Her name and address had been typed, probably on a manual typewriter since some letters were vague and others weren't. She held the envelope a while but finally let it fall to the floor.

She was very close to crying, and that was an activity in which she seldom chose to engage. The letter had been written by an adult, by someone who despised her enough to wait years to embarrass her, someone smart enough to know that while she might have made her peace with loneliness, the terms of any treaty can begin to seem unjust. The "Ms." was particularly snide. "Miss" was still used in Mississippi.

The letter arrived on a Friday. By Tuesday afternoon she was furious. She could not be still. Whenever she walked into the living room and saw the telephone, she wanted to knock it off the end table. She prowled house and garden as long as she could, then she got into her car and drove. West of town, on Beaverdam Road, she passed a cotton picker. When she whipped in front of it, she saw that the driver was Henry King. He waved. She didn't. Twelve or thirteen years ago she'd caught him passing around a drawing of her. In the drawing she was outlandishly large; her figure stood atop a trailer attached to a Mayflower truck. Beneath his work the artist had written, WE CAN MOVE ANYTHING.

She ate supper in Greenville and went to a movie, which she sat through twice. It was midnight when she got home. She bathed and went to bed. Her phone did not ring for almost a month, and then it was only her sister.

•   •   •

Once or twice a year for many years she'd made her trips to Memphis. She usually went once in the fall and once in spring or summer. She'd leave Indianola on a Friday afternoon and when she got to Memphis that evening she'd check in at the Rivermont Holiday Inn. She would eat dinner there, order a bottle of wine for her room, and drink it while she watched the tugboats and barges maneuvering on the river. She might watch a rerun of "Gunsmoke" before she fell asleep.

In the morning, after a breakfast that it took her an hour or more to consume, she'd pack herself into a pair of Levi's and put on an enormous blue sweatshirt and a pair of tennis shoes and the dark glasses she retained for trips to Memphis.

The shop was one of several on Lamar Avenue. It was possible to park right in front of it, but for some reason no one ever did. She always parked her car at a pay lot several blocks away and walked to the shop. Once inside she moved quickly; she never spent more than ten minutes there. Emerging with a large plastic bag, she walked back to her car, doffed her glasses, and headed home. On the way she usually paused for a barbecue plate.

The photos depicted her in all her stealthy pleasures. In one she was leaving the shop, the bag in the crook of her arm. Another, vague and hazy because a windshield lay between the lens and its object, showed her entering Coleman's Barbecue in Tunica, Mississippi. Yet another, snapped from the bluff above the river, showed her with her bare feet up on the balcony railing, a glass in her hand and a wine bottle on the wrought-iron table at her side.

The note that came with the photos was brief. *I guess this is blackmail,* it said. *But if you'll just answer your phone Friday evening at nine o'clock and give me five minutes, I promise I'll send you the negatives.*

This time she did cry. But first she locked the doors and drew the curtains.

•   •   •

"If he asks me again, I'll tell him he's rude. If he says anything the least bit smartassed, I'll ask him who his parents are, and if he refuses to tell me, I'll grab him by the hand and so help me I won't let go until I've dragged him to the owner's office, and we'll see if we can't get to the bottom of it."

That said, Ellis Fuller devoted his attention to his chicken salad. He was unaware that several of the other diners were glancing his way. He was unaware that he'd voiced his thoughts to the air. Unbeknownst to him he'd been doing it for twenty years.

The object of his displeasure was a ten-year-old male who wore an Ole Miss Rebels tee shirt. He was playing the pinball machine that stood near the rear of the cafe. Two weeks ago he'd walked up to the table where Ellis sat every Friday evening from six until eight and in a loud squeaky voice he'd said, "Excuse me, Mr. Fuller." When Ellis looked up, he said, "Are you gay?"

The kid had not noticed him tonight. He finished his chicken salad, ordered dessert and coffee, and ate them in peace. At eight sharp he paid his bill and walked out.

The voice rang out behind him. "Hey, Mr. Fuller, are you gay?"

He quickened his pace and leaped into his Toyota.

In five minutes he was out of town, headed north on 49, his mind on the business before him. The phone he intended to use was mounted on the wall of an abandoned Mr. Quik in Leland. He had chosen this particular phone because the building was on a dark side street, and if anyone from Eureka happened to drive through Leland, it was unlikely that he or she would find the way there.

He parked in black shadows. He pulled up the collar of his windbreaker, seized the paper sack filled with quarters.

The operator came on the line and told him to deposit one eighty-five for the first three minutes. He fed eight quarters into the phone. The operator said, "Fifteen cents credit."

The phone rang twice before Lucille Mitchell said, "Hello."

The lips of Ellis Fuller failed to form words. Last year he'd taken an adult acting class at Delta State in hopes of meeting women; he met many, but whenever had had to act a scene with one of them, he forgot all his lines; he once heard another man in the class whisper, "The only line that guy needs to learn is 'How much?'"

He did not say, "How much?" Instead he said, "May I speak to Ms. Mitchell?"

"This is Lucille Mitchell. Who am I talking to?"

Her voice was thick with authority. He wished his voice sounded like that. He tried to achieve jauntiness. "You're talking to me," he said.

"What do you want?"

"I want to talk to you."

"About what?"

"About a date."

"I'm already seeing somebody."

"Who?"

"Myself."

He resolved to talk tough. The problem was that he'd never talked tough to anyone except himself. He cleared his throat and said, "I still have those negatives."

For a long time she was silent. Then she said, "Why are you doing this to me?"

"I love you."

"Three minutes are up," said the operator. "If you—"

"Get off the line," he yelled. "You goddam intrusive bitch. Get off."

"Jesus . . . Let me know when you're finished."

He was pleased with his outburst. It had been completely spontaneous. "I love you," he said again, and when other words rushed out after those, he made no attempt to stop them. He heard himself speak of an old fixation, of an unathletic youth who languished in the rear of her classroom and, staring as she stood at the lectern, embossed her image on his brain for nocturnal recall. Normally, he said, she had lectured with her arms crossed before her, but toward the end of every period she'd rest both hands on her hips, and when she did that her breasts fought a battle with the buttons on her blouse.

A film of perspiration had formed on his face. He said he could and would tell her more of his passion, but not now. Now he only wanted to arrange a meeting.

She said, "Who are you?"

"You couldn't place my face if you saw it."

"I don't plan to see it."

"I was a good student."

"That rules out almost everybody."

"I want a date."

"Sorry. I sip my misery in private."

He had always known she was miserable. Moisture crept into his eyes. He said, "Ms. Mitchell, I want to tell you something." He said he took antidepressants and saw a therapist once a week and had not turned off his radio since the fall of '85. He said he rose at four because he couldn't sleep and every morning before breakfast he ran fifteen miles. He said he never removed all his clothes except to take a shower.

She made him wait a long time before she said, "I do."

"I knew you did," he said. He felt as if he would choke. When he was once again capable of speech, he said, "Now listen. If you don't agree to meet me for a date, I'll have to send those pictures around."

"Who would you send them to?"

"I'd send them out at random. I'd pick fifteen or twenty names from the Indianola phone book."

"What makes you so sure I wouldn't be secretly pleased to have folks look at those pictures?"

"I'm not sure," he said. "It's entirely possible you would be pleased."

"I wouldn't be," she said. "When and where do you want me to meet you?"

"At the Lake Shore Motel in Lake Village, Arkansas. Check

in next Saturday no later than 10 A.M., and sometime between then and evening I'll contact you."

"That's eight days from now," she said.

He told her he needed some time to collect himself.

•   •   •

The Lake Shore Motel was one long row of rooms with an office at the end. It stood just across the highway from Lake Chicot. When Lucille pulled into the gravel parking lot Saturday morning, the only other vehicle there was a yellow pickup with CAMERON CONSTRUCTION—SHREVEPORT, LA on both doors. She parked her car near the office. Inside she found the desk clerk, a teenaged girl who managed to peel her eyes away from MTV long enough to take her money and assign her room 10. She went back out and moved her car.

The room bore little resemblance to those at the Rivermont. A tear in the lone armchair revealed stuffing the color of gruel, and coffee stains and cigarette burns marred the bedspread. The rug was frayed in the middle as well as at the edges. Shunning contact with fabric, she went into the bathroom and sat down on the edge of the bathtub. The toilet bowl abounded in botanical activity.

She'd spent much of the last week examining old yearbooks, scanning fourteen-year-old faces for signs of psychosis. She was pitted against extreme craziness, of that she harbored no doubts, and as the days passed and Saturday drew closer, anticipation, that ancient stranger, visited her for the first time in ages. She ached to see the face of her antagonist. In her purse now she carried a derringer. Also a children's Polaroid, a steak knife, a pint of Jack Daniel's, and a bottle of sleeping pills she had ground into a fine pink powder.

She was sitting on the tub in a sleazy motel. Her veiny legs tingled. Off and on for a week she'd been beset by spells of weeping preceded or followed by brief epochs of euphoria. The existence of those photos was the last humiliation of her days. She had made up her mind about that.

She rose and went to the window and peeped out at the parking lot, empty now except for her Olds. A red Toyota was passing on the highway. A few minutes later, when she was no longer watching, it went past again.

•　　　　•　　　　•

He cased the place so long he had to stop at the Exxon station and refill his tank. Afterwards he went back and reconnoitered some more. Despite his assertion of fearlessness, policemen terrified him, and he fully expected her to summon them. He would be tried, judged guilty of extortion. Therefore he had arranged the rendezvous for Arkansas. In the Memphis paper he'd read that Cummins Prison was more civilized than Parchman.

When he could put it off no longer for fear that she would leave, he pulled into the parking lot and parked in open daylight by her Olds. He picked up the manila envelope containing the negatives, got out, and knocked on the door to number 10.

She had spied him through the gap in the curtains. He was tall, emaciated, maybe thirty-eight or forty; he wore a pencil-thin moustache and a pair of wire-rimmed glasses. His face did not look familiar.

She made him knock several times. Each knock was fainter than the last. Finally she jerked open the door.

The lips fluttered, the moustache twitched. He shoved the envelope at her. "Here."

She had not believed he'd really bring the negatives. She opened the envelope and looked inside.

"They're all there," he said.

"You probably made other prints."

"Just one extra set."

"For what?"

"For me."

"What do you aim to do with them?"

"Look at them."

"Who are you?"

"My name's Ellis Fuller." He had not intended to tell her that, at least not now, but after what he had done, he deserved no protection. He thought that when he left here he would go and surrender to the Lake Village police. He said, "You taught me in 1962."

His name meant nothing to her. Since she never forgot her students' names, she decided he must be lying. She said, "What do you want with me?"

He could see into the dirty room behind her. The chipped plaster, the rickety nightstand, the old Zenith TV, the cobwebs. When he'd committed each detail to memory, he shifted his gaze to her face, where it lingered on each wrinkle. She must be fifty-five now; her lips were dry and cracked and he bet that like his they had never been kissed. He said, "I want you to hold me."

"Mr. Fuller," she said, "I don't believe that." She turned, walked to the dresser, picked up her purse and jammed the envelope into it. The Jack Daniel's caught her eye. She withdrew it and the bottle of pink powder and, wanting never to see either of them again, set them down on the dresser. Then she walked over to the doorway where he stood. "I thought I might kill you," she said. "If you'd made one wrong move, I believe I really would have done it."

"You probably should have."

"It's nice of you to say that, but I'm glad I didn't. It would've ruined my sleep and my appetite, and those are both very precious to me." She studied his face as she spoke. Still it failed to jog her memory. "Do you want to know," she said, "what else I aimed to do to you, assuming I didn't kill you?"

He knew from the tone of her voice and the look on her face that what she aimed to do to him would not, in the end, have been pleasant. But he also knew that whatever it was, it had never been done to him before. Consequently he was interested. "What?" he said.

"I aimed to seduce you, Mr. Fuller."

She stood back from her words to observe their effect. Once more the moustache quivered.

"And after I'd seduced you," she said, "I'd fix you a great big drink of whiskey mixed with sleeping pills. And when you went to sleep, I'd put my panties on you—they're a black lacy pair that look ridiculous on me but not nearly as ridiculous as they'd look on you—and I'd slip these high-heeled shoes I'm wearing onto your feet, and I'd photograph you. Then I'd pull the panties off and photograph you again in just the shoes. And I'd use those photos to torment you just like you tormented me."

She walked past him out the door. As she was getting into the car, he said, "If you just wanted to embarrass me, why not put me to sleep right away? Why plan to seduce me first?"

He thought he saw the hint of a smile at her mouth. She said, "I'll let you figure that one out." Then she closed her door and drove off.

·   ·   ·

Alan Franconi jogged across the road to the 7-Eleven.

"Well?"

"It's his car," Franconi said. "It's got that big dent in the left fender, and his textbook's laying in the backseat along with those tests he gave us last week."

"Did you see what anybody made?"

"McGregor's was on top. He got a hundred."

McGregor detected general disapproval. He tipped up his Miller and took a big swig, wiped his mouth and said, "Let's smoke another joint."

Ray Jackson said, "Tell me what that queer son of a bitch is doing at a motel in Lake Village?"

"Probably doing something," one of the girls said, "with another queer son of a bitch."

Franconi said, "Wait'll you hear this. There's a real stupid girl in the office. I went in and talked to her and found out the room's in some woman's name."

"Maybe he's in one of the other rooms."

"Nope. As of now that's the only one occupied. His is the only car in the lot anyhow."

At first nobody could believe it. Then, as their imaginations clicked on, everybody believed it, and there was widespread agreement that the situation was rife with possibility. Jackson suggested removing the distributor cap from the Toyota, but Franconi said, "That's infantile, man," and pointed out that anyhow the doors were locked and you couldn't get under the hood from outside. Sheila Tyson suggested calling the principal or the highway patrol.

McGregor said, "Jesus, the guy's got a right to get him some."

"Get some, my ass."

McGregor said, "*He's* the one in the room with a woman, Jackson. You're sitting side the road drunk."

A resolution was passed: they would redefine the human race, thereby excluding McGregor. Then they passed another resolution. They would drive both cars to the motel parking lot, get out and sit on the hoods, and wait till he emerged. When he did, Jackson would shout, "Three cheers for Ellis Fuller," and all of them would join in.

It was six o'clock when they drove to the motel. At nine the night manager came out and ran them off, so they parked across the highway to wait. At eleven the room was still dark, he hadn't come out yet, and everybody needed to get home.

Driving over the Greenville bridge, Jackson said, "You'll never convince me he's been in there with a woman all this time."

McGregor was leaning against the rear door, his head buzzing

from the dope he wasn't used to. He closed his eyes and imagined Mr. Fuller with the woman. He imagined him stroking her
hair, touching her breasts, kissing her thighs and her navel. He
thought about them a long time, until he believed beyond a doubt
in their presence there together.

SARA

MARGARET WINSTON said, "Sara, can I talk to you for a minute?"

Sara laid down a file folder and followed Margaret across the hall, past the new electronic scales, and into her office. Margaret shut the door and sat down. She was thirty-five, tall and black; she wore her hair swept neatly back. She'd once told Sara that when she moved to Mississippi, she had to get used to white people asking, "Is your hair naturally straight?"

Margaret tapped her desk with a Bic. "Lots of times in the last year," she said, "I've wished I hadn't taken this job."

Sara knew what she meant. Two white clerks had quit when Margaret was hired. Betty Waller kept saying, "I pray every day to be delivered from under that dark cloud."

Sara said, "Well, we're a lot more efficient since you came and nobody can claim different."

"You're the only one here who doesn't see me as an enemy. That's why I hate what I have to tell you."

Sara had heard talk of cutbacks in state agencies, but the Health Department was supposed to be safe. Now Margaret was about to fire her. She envisioned herself at home, rocking before the TV, watching "Days of Our Lives." The days of her life would be long. Too long.

Margaret said, "I got authorization to raise one clerk typist to Clerk-Typist I. It's agency policy now to promote staff who have a high-school education. It's going to be Betty, Sara. I'm sorry."

Betty had worked here only two years, and she'd made a mess of the WIC program, a mess Sara helped Margaret resolve. Sara said, "Oh, well . . . I see."

"It's not fair. If you're mad at me, it's understandable."

Sara shrugged. "I'm not mad at you. It's not your fault."

On her coffee break, she sat alone in the lounge, thinking about the way things had worked out. She'd gotten married at sixteen, had her first child at twenty, her second two years later. Raising two children was a full-time job, one that kept her busy for almost twenty years. She'd gone to work here when the younger of her children, her son, went to college; Linda was a junior at Ole Miss then, and they needed the extra money for Paul's tuition.

Back when the kids were both in high school, she'd decided to take the GED. She asked her daughter to help her, so Linda mapped out a study schedule and administered practice tests. She passed them all, though the math gave her fits. Then one morning at breakfast, when they were alone at the table, Jim told her, "If you fail that test, don't let it worry you. You've still got your family." She hadn't even thought of failing. Plenty of stupid people had high-school diplomas, GED certificates; she didn't think she was any dumber than they were. But after Jim said that, she began to fear the exam. The thought of driving home from Delta State, of telling her husband and her children she'd failed—that was more than she could stand. The morning of the test, she woke sick, vomiting. She stayed up ten minutes, then went back to bed. She kept thinking she'd take the test, but she didn't. She kept hoping someone would prod her, but nobody did.

Now she was fifty. It was a little bit late.

•   •   •

Jim Norton was a traditionalist in all things, especially the matter of automobiles. You couldn't have given him a new one; they were all made of plastic these days, and they couldn't stand a good wreck. He owned a '72 Galaxy, a '74 Olds, and a '67 GMC pickup. They'd each chalked up close to 200,000 miles, and he'd make them run till Armageddon if he didn't go broke buying oil.

He'd just finished changing the timing chain on the Olds when he heard a grating noise. It sounded like metal on asphalt, and it was coming down North Avenue at about thirty miles an hour. He rubbed his hands with Go-jo, dried them on a rag, and looked up.

Sara turned into the driveway. The tailpipe of the Galaxy was dragging the pavement, throwing up a steady stream of sparks. She parked and got out. She was redheaded and plump, still cute, Jim thought. He said, "Let me take that sack."

He opened the door for her and carried the Piggly Wiggly bag into the kitchen, where he stood it on a counter.

She said, "I'll start fixing supper."

Outside he surveyed the damage. There was a jagged tear in the green metal skirt beneath the bumper. The tailpipe looked all right, but one of the mounting brackets was missing. She must've run over a curb.

At supper he said, "You didn't hear no funny noises?"

"When?"

"In the car."

"No, but I had the air conditioner on high. Is something wrong?"

"Tailpipe's loose. You'll have to use the Olds in the morning."

He buttered his cornbread and asked if they'd been busy today.

"Not too busy."

"Guess everybody's well."

"I guess so."

"How's your boss?"

She stared at her plate. "All right."

"You know you don't have to keep working under her," he said. "I've told you time and again we don't need your salary anymore. Anytime you want to quit, I'll be overjoyed."

She sliced a chunk of liver. "I don't want to leave them shorthanded."

"Anybody," he said, "could do the work you do." He speared a green pea with his fork.

After supper, he sat at the table, sipping a Coors and watching her wash dishes. When she finished, he said, "You want to go take a walk? We could come back then and look at TV, watch the Braves or whatever."

She tore off a paper towel and dried her hands. "I'm tired," she said. "I think I'll take a bath and go to bed."

"Suit yourself."

It was seven o'clock, plenty of daylight left, so he went out and watered the garden. When he finished, he hopped in the pickup, drove to the liquor store, and bought a fifth of Rebel Yell. At home, he turned on the Braves game. He sipped whiskey and watched TV in the dark. By ten, he felt pretty tight, and he also felt like talking. After one more drink, he called Paul.

When his son answered, Jim said, "Hey. This is the old man."

"Hi, Dad."

"How come you don't call?"

Actually, he knew why. In June, he'd helped Paul move to Fayetteville, Arkansas, where he'd teach at the college. He'd advised him to find an apartment near the school, pointing out that northwest Arkansas got lots of snow. Paul rented a house halfway down a mountain ten miles from town, with a family cemetery fenced off in the yard. Jim cast a look around and said, "You're a fool. All your neighbors are dead." He unloaded the U-Haul and drove off without saying good-bye.

Now Paul said, "You insulted me."

"That's a father's prerogative."

"I'm twenty-nine years old."

"A foolish twenty-nine."

"Damn it, Dad, I'm tired of you talking to me that way."

Jim would've hung up, but there was no one else to call. He and his daughter had been on the outs for several years, ever since she married an Italian.

He said, "Has your house slid into the river?"

"It's still right here."

"How's the dead folks?"

Paul laughed. "Still in the ground. You just can't help it, can you?"

"I'm just doing my parental duty. You're a decent son, all things considered. When's school start?"

"Three weeks."

"Be glad you don't teach in Mississippi. This state's gone to the dogs." He poured another drink. "That damn boycott finally ended. The upshot is, Indianola's fixing to have a—"

"Black superintendent of public schools. I read about it. When do you think you'll have some cotton to gin?"

"Your momma, bless her soul, is down there working under one of 'em. I've told her she ought to quit, but she keeps on. Don't make any sense."

"It must to her."

"Well, it don't to me." He lowered his voice. "She's slipping, son. Today she ran the car over a curb and didn't even know it. Last month, I woke up one morning and the house was full of smoke. She'd left a Teflon pot on the burner and gone to work. Damn near gassed my ass."

"Anybody could've forgotten."

"The women in her family tend to go wild at the end. You never knew your great-grandma, but toward the end of her life she started saving all the table scraps. Filled two footlockers and a suitcase with 'em. Biggest stink you ever smelled. She went out in a straightjacket, convinced she was Della Street."

"Perry Mason's girlfriend?"

"Mrs. Pitts read detective novels. That's what I called you for, son."

Jim's voice was about to crack, but that didn't shame him. He believed in certain values—honesty, decency, family responsibility—and they were worth weeping over.

"If anything happens to me," he said, "I want you to take care of your mother. She'll be completely alone and completely helpless. I want you to promise."

Sara had woken thirsty and walked into the kitchen. For the last few minutes, she'd been standing there listening. Now she heard Jim say, "Don't answer so damn fast. It won't be as easy as you think. You better mull it over. I mean it."

•   •   •

A couple of weeks later, on a Monday morning, he woke with a hangover and a bursting bladder. Stumbling into the bathroom with his eyes closed, he felt the floor tiles squish beneath his feet. He opened his eyes to find the bathroom flooded, the toilet bowl full to the rim. He hissed, "Shit," and pissed in the sink. Then he grabbed the plunger, jammed it into the bowl, and shoved. Water splashed his boxer shorts. He pumped the plunger up and down until he'd cleared the line. Still, he decided, the willow must go. He toweled off his legs and got dressed.

The willow stood in a corner of the yard. Every year, in spring and summer, its roots blocked the sewer line. He'd resisted cutting it down, because it had been here longer than he had. But the problem kept getting worse and worse, and he was tired of toilet worries. He made quick work of the job, severing the trunk with his McCulloch, then carving up the limbs and branches and flinging all the pieces into his pickup. He hauled the whole mess off to the dump, then went back to pull up the stump.

He kept his tractor in the backyard. It was a WD 45 that he'd bought in 1955, paying $1300 for it and a one-row cotton picker. He hadn't farmed since the sixties, but he held on to the tractor for sentimental reasons. He yanked off the tarp, mounted the tractor, and drove it over to the stump, around which he'd already wrapped his chain; while the tractor idled, he hooked the free end of the chain to the tow bar. He climbed back onto the tractor and put it in gear and let off the clutch.

The machine was light; he knew it would buck. But the front end rose much faster than he expected. When it reared up, he panicked and jumped from the seat. He landed on his feet, though the impact forced him to squat. The tractor hadn't tipped over. Feeling foolish, he started to stand.

Pain speared his spine. His legs twitched, crumbled.

He'd had lower back troubles before but never like this. White spots jigged before his eyes, and his stomach rose and fell. He was about to black out. Using the last of his strength, he crawled off into the bushes.

He didn't want anybody to drive by and find him disabled.

•   •   •

He was full of Flexeril, Percodan too. A broad nylon band corseted his waist. Cords ran from metal hooks on the corset to the foot of the bed, where four lead weights hung suspended. Seeing him this way made Sara feel odd. He'd never been sick before, except for a few colds, which he cured by getting mad and chopping wood.

He crooked a finger. She leaned closer.

"Insurance," he mumbled. "Got a shit-load. Don't worry."

His eyeballs rolled. In seconds he was sleeping.

She went home and fixed a tuna-fish sandwich for her first supper alone in years. During the fall, when Jim ginned cotton, she cooked at home, drove two hot plates to the gin, and they ate together in the room overlooking the scales, while saws and suction pipes threw up a din that rattled the walls and made her hands tremble.

She ate her sandwich and washed the plate. Then she sat down on the living room couch, beneath Pinky and Blue Boy, and tried to think what to do. Gin season would start any day—Jim'd had his crew on standby since Friday—and if there was no one to run the gin, the farmers would go elsewhere. The men on the crew were mostly kids, eighteen- and nineteen-year-olds who he said could barely tell cotton from foam rubber. The doctor had said he could be in traction for up to three weeks.

If they were churchgoers, she knew, her house would be swarming with folks wanting to help. But they hadn't attended in almost twenty years. In 1967, he'd accused the preacher of stealing church funds, and when the man called him a liar, he punched him. It turned out the preacher had filched the money, but in the initial turmoil everyone sided with him, prompting Jim to wash his hands of religion. When the new preacher came by to witness, Jim said, "If you want to be a witness, go find a trial." That was the last time anyone from First Baptist set foot in her house. She could've returned to church on her own, but she knew he expected her not to.

She'd just about decided to phone Paul when she recalled the conversation she'd overheard the other day. It had nagged her, lurking around in the back of her mind, ever since. She put down the phone and sat there a while longer, considering some possibilities. Around six-thirty, she phoned James Barton.

He was retired, almost seventy now, but he used to run the gin in Inverness. She told him what had happened and asked if he knew anyone who could take over until around the first of September.

James said, "I could do it, Sara."

"I was hoping you'd say that," she said. "You're sure about it?"

"Hell yes. I'd love to." He promised to pick up the key the next morning.

That night she parched peanuts. She carried a pan of them into the living room where, for the first time in a long time, she watched TV until ten.

•   •   •

"James Barton." He shook his head, then winced. The slightest movement hurt him. "Did you happen to notice his right hand? It's got two fingers on it. The left one's more prosperous—it's got three. That's from reaching into a lint cleaner. James is a mite absentminded."

"I'm sorry," she said. "I didn't know."

"So much can go wrong around a gin," he informed her. "Sometimes you'll find a cotton sack buried in a trailer full of cotton. You've got to keep an eye on your suction man, make sure he don't feed nothing foreign up the pipe—it could burn the whole gin down. You've got to ride herd on your yard man, else he'll let the cotton stand out and get wet. James is just too batty to be entrusted with all that. He can't keep track of his own fingers." He shook his head again, less vigorously this time. "You messed up bad," he told her.

Sara stood near the foot of the bed. For the last ten minutes he'd berated her nonstop.

"Well," she said, "I thought I ought to do something."

"You should've asked me first."

"You were asleep."

"You should've waited till I woke up. I want you to go home and call James and tell him I got somebody else. Then I want you to call Linwood Hart at Twin Bayou and ask him to loan me Bobby Simpkin."

James had come for the key this morning at seven. He wore coveralls and work shoes and a red-and-grey Continental Gin cap. He said he was eager to look the place over. Before leaving, he said, "Thanks for calling me, Sara. I sure miss ginning."

Sara said, "Jim, I can't tell him that."

"The hell you can't."

"Please. He's been so nice."

"Tell him." He clamped his eyes shut.

She walked over to the window. She stood there awhile, staring across the street at Hull Brothers Clinic, letting the sunlight warm her. In a minute she peeked over her shoulder. His eyes were still closed. She sat down in an armchair and leafed through the *Enterprise Tocsin*. At five till one, she stood and told him good-bye. He said nothing.

All afternoon she dreaded her return to the hospital. He'd ask if she'd phoned James. She'd have to say no. She felt sick when five o'clock came.

She drove home and ate another tuna-fish sandwich. Then she washed her plate. After that, she picked up her purse and headed for the front door, but when she reached the living room, the couch looked inviting. She sank onto the cushions. Sitting there, she remembered how pleasant last night had been, just her crunching peanuts and drinking tea and gazing at the TV. She used to hunker on the floor, watch TV with the kids, shows like "Andy Griffith" and "The Lucy Show" and, later, "Here Come the Brides." Even after Paul and Linda entered high school, the three of them often watched "M.A.S.H." But the last ten years, this room had been Jim's. He sat there every night, drinking on the couch, the lights turned off, the sound on the TV turned down. She tried her best to stay away.

Now light bathed the room. The curtains were open, and she could see all the cars on North Avenue and the big red sign above Fred's Dollar Store. She pulled off her shoes and got comfortable. If the hospital phoned, she would claim she had a virus.

The hospital didn't phone. At six the next morning, after a restful night, she crawled out of bed, slipped on her bathrobe, and went outside for the paper. The carrier had left it near the tractor, which still stood chained to the stump. She scanned the sky, saw clouds bunching up over Leland. She laid the paper on the hood of Jim's pickup, walked into the backyard, grabbed a corner of the tarp and dragged it into the front yard, where she threw it over the tractor.

She ate breakfast and read the paper. Walking through the living room on her way to take her bath, she let her eye light on the stereo. She dropped to her knees and pawed through the records, shoving aside Jim's Carter Family LPs and *Johnny Cash at Folsom Prison,* until she found the album she wanted. She harbored a secret fondness for rock and roll. Jim had forbidden the kids to play it, but anytime he left the house they'd seized the chance to rattle the walls. She voiced no objections, just stood there cooking and tapping her toe and looking out the window in case Jim came home. One day Linda said, "Tell the truth, Mother. You love it." She shook her head no.

She put *Green River* on the turntable. The first chords of "Bad Moon Rising" summoned images of the late sixties, of the summer when she and her children drove to Greenwood almost every day. Jim had just bought the gin, and he needed electrical parts. She drove fast so there'd be time for lunch at the Crystal Grill. She always said, "Don't tell your daddy we ate out." They never asked why. They knew he opposed frivolity.

She bathed and dressed, fixed her sandwich and stuck it in a brown paper bag. On her way to work she passed the hospital. The parking lot looked crowded.

•   •   •

She was typing up reports for the sanitary engineer when Margaret said, "Sara, line two."

She picked up the phone. "Hello?"

He hissed. "Where the hell are you?"

"Here . . . I'm here. Where are you?"

"At the pay phone." He sounded as if his jaws were locked. "Come get me."

"But the doctor—"

"Damn the doctor. Listen . . . last night I was watching TV, and Nell Westbrook came in and cut it off and ordered me to go to sleep. Then I was trying to read and she ripped the paper out of my hand and cut off the light. I wake up this morning and some girl's pulling down my drawers, and when I ask her what the hell she's up to, she says, 'Time for a shot,' and stabs me with a needle. Piss on this. I'll recover at home. Come get me."

"You're supposed to be in traction. A back injury's nothing to fool with."

"I said come get me."

She felt fortified by South Central Bell. Half a mile of cable reinforced her. "You get back in bed," she said. "For your own good. Bye."

She went back to work. By midafternoon, she'd almost decided to go home at five and unplug the phone. That prospect made her feel light-headed, the way she'd felt a few years ago when she took high-blood-pressure medicine. In the end, she talked herself into going to the hospital. She found him in the traces, harnessed-up and snoring. She tiptoed out of the room and sat down on a bench in the hall, where she scribbled him a note. *I was here. Sara.* She slinked into his room and propped the note against a plastic water pitcher.

When she walked into the house, the phone was ringing. James Barton.

"Hey, Sara," he hollered. "Just ginned my first bale in six years. Roy Washington brought in a trailer."

"That's great," she said. "How's it feel?"

"Feels real good. This gin's something else—runs like a toy train, and it's cleaner than my kitchen. That husband of yours, he's the best damn ginner around."

Sara traced a circle on the windowsill. "Yes," she said. "I guess he does know how to run a gin."

•   •   •

That evening she watched *Cool Hand Luke* on WTBS. The young Paul Newman looked a lot like Jim used to. He was mischievous in the movie, and that was exactly how Jim had seemed to her when she was sixteen. She'd grown up on the farm next to his and had known him all her life. She'd been there the day he and Alvin Wade drilled a hole beneath the pulpit and then crawled under the church and loosed a jar of bees in the middle of Brother Burke's sermon. She remembered the day he ran away from school three times; the last time, his father found him in the hayloft, eating a pound cake he'd swiped from Blanchard's Bakery.

That kind of behavior appealed to a lot of girls, she knew, especially the shy ones like her. He was three years older than her, and dating him was a big thing. He waited for traffic lights to turn red so he could run them. He played pranks, cracked jokes, made her laugh. But after their marriage, all the laughing stopped. He tried farming with his father, but he and Mr. Norton couldn't get along, and whenever they battled, he brought his anger home. He'd have spells where he'd go two or three weeks without saying more than two or three words.

When his father died and left him the farm, his humor improved. He hatched plans for rebuilding the barn, for converting half the cotton acreage to rice and soybeans. She listened and nodded. Then she went and played with her children.

Now there was the TV, this big empty house. She watched movies until midnight and fell asleep on the couch.

• • •

Thursday morning she woke feeling broken. There was a crick in her neck, and her shoulder hurt. She'd had a terrible dream, in which Jim developed spinal meningitis and died. On the morning of his funeral, she overslept. She arrived at the cemetery just as the preacher—the same one he'd punched—heaved a spadeful of dirt into the grave.

She dressed quickly and drove to the hospital. In the hall outside his room, she heard him say, "I don't want a damn bath. Get away."

She turned and walked out before anybody saw her.

•   •   •

Margaret sat at the table in the lounge and watched Sara draw coffee from the urn. "You look tired," she said.

Sara sat down with her Styrofoam cup. "I stayed up too late."

"How's your husband?"

"He's all right."

"Still in the hospital?"

"Yes."

Margaret tapped the Formica with a long, polished nail. "Well," she said. "I suppose I'd better go back to work."

"Would you . . . would you like to come over tonight? To my house?"

If the invitation surprised her, Margaret concealed it. "Sure," she said. "What time?"

"Well . . . maybe seven?"

"Seven's fine."

Later, at Piggly Wiggly, Sara bought a can of Planter's mixed nuts and a one-pound bag of Ruffles potato chips. She drove home and bathed and ate her sandwich. At six she called the hospital and asked a nurse to tell Jim she was sick. She filled a salad bowl with chips, dumped the nuts into a smaller bowl, then carried them both into the living room and sat down to wait.

At seven sharp, Margaret rang the doorbell. She wore jeans and a maroon-and-white Howard University tee shirt. She handed Sara a huge brown sack with something heavy inside it. Sara pulled out a green gallon jug of Chablis.

"Wine?"

"Oops," Margaret said. "You don't drink?"

"I don't have anything against it. It's just . . . Oh, I might as well try some."

In the kitchen, she took out two glasses. Examination of the wine bottle revealed that it had a cork instead of a cap. She dug Jim's corkscrew out of a drawer. She'd never used a corkscrew before, but she studied it until she had it figured out. Only one cork fragment ended up in the wine.

Margaret was sitting on the couch, flipping through a photo album that lay on the coffee table. "Thanks," she said when Sara handed her the glass. "Is this your son?"

The picture had been taken the day Paul graduated from Ole Miss. He stood before Tad Smith Coliseum, clad in black cap and gown, his arm around Sara.

"Yes—that's Paul. He hasn't got a beard anymore."

She turned the page. "This is my daughter, Linda. And that's her husband—Mike Niccolossi. He's a doctor. And that's my grandson. His name's Philip."

"They're an attractive family. Where do they live?"

"Atlanta."

"Do you see them often?"

"Well, they're pretty busy." Sara sat down in an armchair. "And you know, Atlanta's not really so close."

Margaret sipped her wine, so Sara did the same. It tasted awful. Sour, stale. She said, "This tastes nice."

After that, neither spoke for a while. The silence dismayed Sara. All afternoon she'd looked forward to the evening, when she'd have somebody to talk to. Now she could think of nothing to say. The gulf between her and Margaret loomed shoreless.

Finally Margaret said, "Well, Sara, I'm moving away."

"When?"

"In about six months."

"I'm sorry. I'll be sorry when you leave."

Margaret laughed. "I doubt anybody else shares your feelings. Betty'll dance on her desk." She set her glass on the table. "David, my husband, is going to be a resident at a hospital in D.C. We moved down here mainly because he was born in Greenwood—his grandmother still lives there—and there's only one other black doctor in town, a seventy-year-old man who's semiretired. David saw a need. But our daughter'll be school age in two more years, and I refuse to send her to school down here."

"I guess you'd have better schools in a big city."

"Yes. But it's not just that. I feel like I'm on display here. I can't go into Piggly Wiggly without people staring at me, and about once a week somebody stops me in the street and tells me how pretty my teeth are." She shook her head. "I wasn't prepared for this. David convinced me things had changed a lot more than they have. And then too, I miss everything you can do in a place like D.C."

Sara said, "Sometimes I've thought living in a city might be nice. I guess the biggest one I've ever seen's Memphis."

"Isn't Atlanta bigger than Memphis?"

"I haven't actually been to Atlanta."

Margaret said, "Did your daughter just move there?"

"No, she's been there about five years."

"Five *years?*"

Sara partook of the wine. The second sip tasted as bad as the first. She said, "The thing is, Linda married a Catholic."

Margaret stared at her.

"Jim doesn't much like Catholics. So we don't visit."

Margaret stared a while longer. Then she said, "Excuse me." She rose and walked into the kitchen and returned carrying the bottle, which she stood on the coffee table. "You don't visit your daughter because of religious reasons," she said, sitting down. "Yet I once heard Betty remark that you and your husband don't attend church."

"That's so."

"Isn't that . . . isn't that a little strange, Sara? I mean if you were really devout Baptists or something, maybe I could understand it. Maybe. But that's not the case, is it?"

"No."

"What we're talking about's just bigotry."

Sara said, "Oh, Margaret, I don't know if I know what that word means. I just know I don't see my children, and my son-in-law's afraid to let my grandson visit. I haven't been to church in almost twenty years, and I don't think I have a friend in the world. My husband's in the hospital, and bad as it sounds and strange as I feel about it, I think I like having him gone."

Margaret leaned over and refilled her wine glass. She took a sip from it and set it on the table. Then she crossed her legs.

"I'm here," she told Sara. "I'm listening."

·   ·   ·

When she woke the next morning, her mouth was dry, but otherwise she felt fine. She made the bed, threw open the curtains. Dust crystals danced in the light.

In the kitchen she spied the wine bottle. Two-thirds empty, and it was partly her doing. She felt something kin to pride. When she sat down to eat, she thought about last night. She'd told Margaret she wished she had an education. She told her about overhearing Jim's conversation with Paul. She said she thought things might be a little different if she could hang a diploma on the wall. Margaret said, "A B.S. won't keep a man from doing his best to BS you. David and I go a few rounds." Sara said, "I was trained not to fight." Margaret said, "Me too. But I broke training." They both laughed. Sara said, "You know what? I love rock and roll." She played *Tarkio Road*.

When she walked into the office, Margaret smiled at her, and later, while Sara worked on some requisition forms, Margaret walked by and laid a hand on her shoulder. For the rest of the morning, Betty Waller glared at her.

She drove home to eat lunch. The second she opened the door, Jim hollered, "Sara?" She felt like she had in grade school when the teacher, rumored ill, showed up after all. She'd thought she had time on her hands. Now he'd have his hands on her time. She dropped her purse on the couch, then walked down the hall.

He lay in bed, a Sprite can balanced on his chest. He said, "I got a little surprise this morning."

"Me too," she said. "I mean, you know, I'm surprised to find you home."

"I bet you are," he said. "I made 'em bring me. I'd intended to apologize for the way I talked to you at the hospital—I figured you meant well asking James, and I figured you were staying away out of sheepishness at screwing things up. It never crossed my mind you wouldn't do what I asked you. I called the gin this morning expecting Bobby Simpkin and who do I hear but the Man with Few Fingers. What in the hell's got into you?"

"What'd you say to James?"

"I said he could go on home. Then I called Twin Bayou and asked Bobby if . . . Why are you looking at me like that?"

"You don't know, do you?"

"If I knew, I wouldn't ask."

She said, "When you called James and told him you didn't have any use for him, did you ever stop to think how it might make him feel?"

He swigged Sprite and mopped his mouth with the back of his hand. "Ought to make him feel relieved," he said. "Let him hang around much longer, he'd start losing his toes."

"You're mean," she said. "Just out-and-out mean."

She turned and walked out of the house.

•   •   •

About two that afternoon, his bladder had reached flood stage, so he heaved himself out of bed and hobbled down the hall to the bathroom. When he flushed, the toilet filled up and almost overflowed. He didn't give a damn. He hurt too bad to care. In bed, he swallowed a Percodan and passed out.

He'd had lots of funny dreams in the hospital—the result, he knew, of his taking pain-killers—so when he heard the spitting engine, he thought it was a nightmare. But he could see the ridged plaster on the ceiling, and if he could see that, his eyes must be open. He sat up in bed. The noise refused to subside.

He staggered outside in his boxer shorts. Sara was sitting on the tractor, her hands clenching the wheel. She wore a dark blue shirt and Jim's straw hat, and she was looking over her shoulder at the stump. When she turned around, she saw Jim.

All his life he had thought himself a good man. He'd told as much of the truth as he knew, and he would have died for eight or nine principles. But right now he hated his wife. He'd tear her off the tractor if he had to.

"Get off," he hollered. "Get off my goddam tractor." He drew himself upright and advanced.

Then he saw her face. She was staring down the hood of the tractor as if it were the barrel of a shotgun.

He got out of her way.

THE LODE SENTRY

WHEN Joe Doss opens the front door, Faubus springs up off the carpet. For an instant Joe and the huge golden retriever glare at each other. Finally, Faubus utters a low growl and ambles away. Joe goes then to the rubber plant, kneels down beside it and examines the dark green leaves, running his fingers over them carefully. The rubber plant, which was once a present for his first wife, Lyna Lee, is seven years old. Last week Faubus tipped the plant over and trampled it. Now there is a brown spot on one of its leaves. Joe checks the soil. He decides the plant won't need watering tonight.

In the kitchen he finds his mother-in-law Noreen churning grapes. "Them folks from Canada called here today," she says. "I told them where they could get hold of you."

A firm in Quebec is bidding against the Tradewind Corporation for the rights to the Lode Sentry. "I talked to them," Joe says. "Where's Sue?"

"She's out in the back picking grapes. How much of an offer are they making?"

"Not enough."

Noreen shoots a stream of tobacco spit into a McDonald's cup. Joe feels his stomach start to crawl toward his throat. He has never liked the sight of tobacco spit, and now there are cups of it all over the house. "You a fool, Joe Doss," Noreen informs him. "You a fool if you don't take whatever they'll give you. Poor old Merl worked like a mule ever day of his life and never did make—"

Joe doesn't wait to hear the rest. He knows exactly what Merl made. Merl made zero, Merl made zilch, which is why Merl's widow has to live here right now.

Sue is standing at a trellis, pulling grapes off the vine. A chaw of tobacco swells her left jaw. On the ground beside her rests a red bucket. Sue's brother owns a small vineyard over in Arkansas, and he taught her to grow grapes and make her own wine. Fleetingly, Joe recalls the time he harbored hopes of putting a satellite dish in his backyard. "Well," Sue says, "how much?"

Joe pulls off a couple of grapes and puts them in his mouth. "Not nearly enough," he says between chews. "And they're just like Tradewind—they insist on having all the production rights."

"How much did you make fixing TVs last year?"

"Maybe fourteen thousand."

"Is either company offering more than that?"

"A little bit. But that's not the point."

"Tell me what the point is."

"The man who invented the paper clip made a million dollars. The man who corrugated the paper clip made eight million."

"What's that got to do with you?"

"The first guy did damn well, but the second one did better because he had a royalty deal, Sue. I want to license a manufacturer on a straight royalty basis. Say I get five dollars for every unit they produce. If they produce a million units, that's five million dollars. Even if they only produce a hundred thousand, that's still half a million."

"It looks to me like we ought to get something out of it while we can. If we don't hurry up and take one of the offers, they may back off. Then all the time you spent building the Lode Sentry was just wasted."

Sue has just voiced Joe's greatest fear: that in the end he'll have nothing to show for his ingenuity. But he's convinced the Lode Sentry is worth more than anyone cares to admit. "I just don't want somebody else living it up off me," he tells Sue.

Sighing, Sue bends and picks up her bucket. "Well," she says, "nobody is, Joe. Rest assured."

She turns and goes inside, leaving Joe alone at the vine.

•   •   •

Noreen is not Sue's mother.

Noreen is Lyna Lee's mother. When Noreen's husband died, he left her deeply in debt, so she sold her house and came to live with Joe and Lyna Lee. Not too long after that, Lyna Lee was killed in an automobile accident.

They had been on the verge of starting a family. After the accident, Joe sat on the couch for hours at a stretch, thinking how much easier it would have been if Lyna Lee had left him a child. Instead, she had left him a mother-in-law.

And every time Joe worked up the nerve to suggest they make different living arrangements, Noreen seemed to bring Lyna Lee's name up. Before long, it became apparent to him that she was a good deal smarter than he was. She knew how to hold a strategic position. He kept promising himself he would suggest that she move, but he put it off and put it off, until one night he realized the two of them had been living there together for over three years. When he realized that, he drove to Greenville and got drunk. The next morning he woke up in a strange apartment with a woman who claimed to be his wife.

When he expressed strong doubts, the woman produced a piece of paper and read from it. "State of Arkansas. County of Chicot. You are hereby licensed to celebrate the rites of matrimony between Mr. Joseph Paul Doss and Miss Susan Johnson Withrow, and for so doing, this shall be your warrant."

It started coming back to him. He remembered that it had

seemed like a good idea at the time, a way to tunnel under Noreen. "Arkansas?" he said.

"You have to get a blood test in Mississippi. In Arkansas you don't. We drove across the bridge to Lake Village."

Joe reached for the piece of paper.

"No sir," Susan Johnson Withrow said, hopping out of bed. "Keep your paws off it for the time being. You're a grown man. You knew what you were doing."

"I was drunk."

"Well, you knew what you were doing when you got drunk," she said. "Now. Where exactly do we live?"

•   •   •

Sue was a waitress at a truckstop in Greenville. She was in her midthirties, not really bad looking except for her lips, which were permanently puckered, shaped in an O. "The one thing you never do," she told Joe while she boxed up her belongings, "is call me Pucker. Just about anything else I'll put up with."

The note of resignation in her voice suggested she had put up with everything else.

On the way home Joe considered telling her about Noreen but finally decided against it. Maybe the shock of walking in and discovering her husband came with a mother-in-law would bring her back down to reality.

Sue and Noreen eyed each other askance for a couple of days. Joe felt sure one or both of them would leave. Then Noreen said, "It's been lonesome around the house with nobody here save me and Joe Doss."

"My mother passed away when I was twelve," Sue said. "This is just a golden chance to start over."

A couple of weeks later Sue and Noreen put the trellises up in the backyard and planted grapes. When Joe got home and saw what they had done, he said, "That's where I aimed to put my satellite dish."

"There's nothing in the world," Sue told him, "any better than the wine you make from the brass scuppernong."

Noreen said she had never been big on drinking, but knowing she had helped make the wine herself and wasn't pouring money into the big-time liquor industry would make a large difference, she believed.

She played the flute. In the evening after supper, she gave Noreen lessons. They were soon playing bluegrass melodies, Noreen accompanying on a secondhand instrument Sue had bought her at the pawnshop.

"I never had much use for flutes," Noreen said, "until I found out you could toot bluegrass on one."

"I'll tell you how I discovered it," Sue said. "I was in the band at Conway High School, and I'd always loved bluegrass. Well, one day I was feeling lonesome, so I just started blowing 'Foggy Mountain Breakdown,' just like that, and I've had hours and hours of pleasure ever since."

Joe had once tried to learn to play the harmonica but had quit after a few days because he knew he would never do it well. Noreen and Sue didn't care how badly they played. Every time they finished a number, Joe would hear them giggling, congratulating each other on their performances. The pleasure they took in playing their flutes puzzled him. He supposed he envied them a little bit.

He thought that since he had a wife, he ought to get laid regularly, but that proved impossible. Sue started chewing tobacco, something she said she had done in her girlhood but had given up several years ago. "I let society force me to quit," she said, "but I'm through with that now." She wouldn't make love unless Joe first spent some time kissing her. "If you don't kiss me," she said, "it makes it all feel impersonal." Joe said he would be happy to kiss her if she wouldn't chew tobacco. "You'll have to learn to love me for what I am," she said. "It may take a while, Joe, but you and me have got plenty of time. I don't mind waiting a little longer."

Having Sue for a wife, Joe decided, was harmful to his nature. He thought of asking for a divorce, but Sue seemed so happy just to be married that he couldn't bring himself to do it. And anyway, a divorce would probably cost him everything he and Lyna Lee had worked and paid for together.

He began to feel hopeless.

•   •   •

One night he came home and found a puppy in the house. "His name," Sue told him, "is Faubus. I named him after Orval Faubus, who used to be governor of Arkansas. He was my momma's all-time favorite politician."

Faubus' growth progressed geometrically. Each evening when Joe came home, the dog seemed twice as large as he had been the day before. The bigger he grew, the clumsier he became. He was always blundering into furniture, sending lamps crashing with a swipe of his tail. One night he lumbered into the living room and upset a cup of tobacco spit, which Noreen, who had begun to chew too, had left on the arm of the couch.

Joe sat watching the brown stain spread over the cushion. From the kitchen came the shrill sound of "Rocky Top," piped loudly off-key by Sue and Noreen. Joe stood up and went outside.

In the corner of the yard his Tradewind travel trailer was parked. He and Lyna Lee had bought the trailer secondhand, hoping to take a vacation trip that never materialized. Joe unlocked the trailer. He ran a power cord into the house—to draw electricity to the trailer—then sat down inside the Tradewind and closed his eyes, enjoying the peace.

He began spending his evenings in the trailer. Sue and Noreen didn't seem to mind. In fact, they didn't really seem to notice.

One evening in late May the trailer felt stuffy, so he turned the air on. He already had the lights and the coffee maker on, and a few minutes later, when he plugged in the radio and switched it on, the power went off. It was completely dark inside the trailer. He had no flashlight. It took him half an hour to paw around and find the breaker switch, which turned out to be inconveniently placed, in a corner of the bathroom cabinet.

The same thing happened the next night and again a couple of nights later. Joe was intrigued. He called several other people who owned Tradewinds and found out they all had the same problem. You could never be certain how much was too much, everybody said, until the breaker switch had already been tripped.

"I think I can stop it," he told Sue and Noreen at breakfast one morning. "All I'd have to do would be rig something up that could monitor the current and shut everything off right before the load got to be too much. That way, you wouldn't ever have to fool with the breaker switch. Since you'd be standing right by the outlet, you could just unplug whatever you'd just plugged in and everything else would come right back on.

"And Jesus—there's half a million Tradewinds in circulation, every one of which has the same problem. And so do some of the other makes. Plus, there's no reason why you couldn't adapt this kind of energy regulator for household use. I could make a lot of money."

Sue said, "How much?"

"I don't know. Maybe several hundred thousand. Maybe more. It'd depend on the deal you struck."

Slow grins spread across Sue's and Noreen's faces.

"Aw, Joe," Sue said, shaking her head and picking up the newspaper.

"Joe Doss has trained his sights on the stars," Noreen snickered.

Joe got the impression that if he had said twenty thousand, they would have been interested.

Despite their lack of interest, he continued to think about the problem. If nothing else, thinking about it gave him something pleasant to do. In the evenings, while Sue and Noreen tended the grapes and played their flutes, he sat in the Tradewind. Pondering.

One Saturday he drove to Greenville and bought some materials at Tri-State Electronics. He worked on the device each night. After several weeks of trial and error, he came up with something he believed would do the job. The device was simple enough: a metal box with an amp meter and an auxiliary contact inside it; he thought that if he set the auxiliary contact slightly below the circuit trip-point, the contacts would make before an overload occurred, opening a contactor and shutting off power.

He hooked the device up in the Tradewind. Then he turned on the lights and the air. Then the hot plate. Nothing happened.

The radio.

The trailer went dark.

When he unplugged the radio, everything else came back on.

Nine months later he owned U.S. patent number 49373222. He named his invention the Lode Sentry.

•   •   •

When Joe opens the front door, Sue is waiting for him. Today he received two calls at work: one from the firm in Quebec and one from the Tradewind Corporation itself. He can tell from Sue's face that both callers first tried to phone him at home. "What do you aim to do?" says Sue.

"Stand pat."

"Are they offering more money?"

"A little."

"How much?"

"A whole lot less than the Lode Sentry's worth."

"You don't think you ought to consult anybody else in your family?"

Joe is about to say no when he notices the rubber plant. Its leaves are glossy tonight, shinier than he has ever seen them.

He touches the leaves and finds them sticky. "What's been done to this plant?" he says.

"Oh, today somebody at the Wal-Mart told Noreen you could make a rubber plant look better if you put a little something oily on it."

Joe is suspicious of such country wisdom. "What did she put on it?" he says. "It's sticky now."

"I don't know. Some kind of oil, I guess."

"Noreen," Joe calls. "Come here a minute."

When Noreen appears, Joe asks her what she put on the plant. "I just put some mayonnaise on it," she says. "Ain't it pretty this evening?"

"I despise you," Joe says.

Noreen's old face collapses. Breaking into tears, she whirls and runs from the room.

"If my daddy had talked to his momma-in-law that way," Sue says, "my mother would have left him. Stone cold. I know that for a fact."

Joe starts to point out that Sue is somewhat confused—Noreen isn't really his mother-in-law, she's his ex-mother-in-law, and he has been feeding her for nearly eight years—but he decides it would be pointless. And anyway, he regrets what he said: Noreen knows he looks after the plant because it belonged to Lyna Lee; she was probably just trying to help.

He trudges into the kitchen and dampens a rag to try and clean off the leaves of the rubber plant.

Sue gets down on her knees to help him. "All I ever wanted in my life," she says, "was to have a house of my own and a family and dog. That doesn't mean anything to you."

"This particular family and dog," Joe says, "they're not the ones I expected, Sue. And the house I can't hardly recognize. It's a combination wine cellar and Grand Ole Opry."

Quietly, Sue gets up and leaves him alone.

Joe goes out to the Beer Smith Lounge and pours down nine or ten Millers. While he drinks he thinks about his life. Lyna Lee left him the rubber plant and Noreen. The rubber plant was nice, but Noreen has probably killed it. Because of Noreen he went out and got drunk and woke up with Sue. Because of Sue he now has grapes in his backyard where he would like a nice satellite dish. He has a big dog, bad bluegrass at night. Sue and the grapes and Noreen and Faubus are each okay in their own right, but Joe has been tired of them for a long time. The only thing in his life that means anything to him, he decides, is the Lode Sentry, for which no one will give him a royalty deal. He aches for continuous returns.

When he gets back home, he finds Sue and Noreen sitting side by side on the couch. Faubus lies on the floor next to Sue's foot. Seeing them there, all rowed up as if posed for a photo, Joe suddenly realizes that they are his family, the only family he has, and for an instant he feels scared, dependent.

"We've been talking," Sue says. "First off, I think you ought to admit I didn't trick you into marrying me."

"I admit it," Joe admits.

"Right when you did it, you wanted to."

"I know."

"If you want to now, I'll let you divorce me."

Joe's head is fuzzy from a beer or two too many. He's certain he didn't hear right. "What?" he says.

"D-I-V-O-R-C-E," Noreen spells. "Like in the song the hairdresser from Tupelo recorded."

"Tammy Wynette," Sue says. "But it all hinges on one condition."

Hinges and conditions and Tammy Wynette. Joe sinks into a chair.

"Don't you want to know what the condition is?" says Sue.

Joe thinks vaguely that maybe he doesn't. Maybe he ought to go to bed.

"Tell him," says Noreen.

"I know they're not offering you much for the Lode Sentry," Sue says. "But I want fifteen thousand dollars. Seventy-five hundred for me and seventy-five hundred for Noreen. We want to buy a housetrailer. We can park it at my brother's place in Arkansas."

It takes several seconds to sink in.

When it does sink in, Joe cries, "You mean you want to leave me?"

"Don't you want to be rid of us?"

It isn't that he doesn't. "Well," he says slowly, "it's not that I don't."

"Then what is it?"

Joe isn't sure what it is. He tries to think about it, but if his mind knows the answer, it's hiding it from him. "I guess I just hadn't counted on you being quite so ready to leave," he finally says, and it occurs to him this may be the truth. "I mean, I thought you liked being married."

"I do. I imagine I'll get married again."

"If you can do it once," Noreen says, "you can do it twice. You've proved yourself, honey."

"If that's the way you two feel," Joe says, aware that he sounds sullen, "just go on and get the hell out. I never wanted either one of you here in the first place. The hell with you."

"What about the money?" says Sue. "Can you get that much for the Lode Sentry?"

The money. For a second Joe feels humiliated. He wishes she had asked five times as much. She's selling her rights to him, and he wishes she valued them more highly. Then he realizes there's a second way to see this. He's buying her and Noreen off, and they can be had for seventy-five hundred apiece.

Here and now, as he half-sits, half-lies in his armchair, while his ex-mother-in-law and soon to be ex-wife stare at him, he understands that market value is a relative thing. Sue and Noreen have set their market value at fifteen thousand dollars. Relative to that, the Lode Sentry's market value is astronomical.

Joe Doss tells himself that in the future he won't let anyone else estimate his worth. It's demeaning, he thinks, and it ought to be a private matter anyhow, a simple question of how pleasant his days are.

"Joe," Sue says, "can you get that much?"

"How about six thousand apiece?"

"No."

"Sixty-five hundred? And I'll toss in two sets of bedclothes and half the silverware?"

"That won't do."

"Suppose I just give you the Lode Sentry."

"I don't want it. I want what I said."

"Okay," Joe says, "I guess I can get fifteen thousand."

Sue and Noreen glance at each other. Little smiles romp at the corners of their mouths. Joe imagines they'll steal off to the kitchen in a minute and slap palms.

"But it hinges on one condition," he says.

They watch him suspiciously, faces gone ferrety.

"I want it in writing," he says.

Words on paper, he remembers, often prove useful.

•   •   •

Sue and Noreen and Faubus are gone. The Lode Sentry is currently in production. Joe accepted Tradewind's offer, the same one they made the day he found the mayo on the rubber plant. He sold all production rights to the Lode Sentry for a flat $300,000. He knows that financially he was cheated: Tradewind claimed they planned to manufacture the Lode Sentry only as standard equipment for the trailers they built from now on; it wouldn't be worthwhile, they said, to produce the device for over-the-counter sales, which was why they couldn't offer the kind of deal Joe wanted. Joe, however, knows perfectly well that they wouldn't have sought all the production rights—and paid $300,000 for them—if they never intended to manufacture the Lode Sentry for a wider market. But while he would have liked to keep everybody honest, he now believes that is too big a task for one man.

In his backyard stands the satellite dish he wanted so long. The dish is aimed at the heavens. He has Sony consoles in three different rooms.

He spends very little time, though, enjoying his luxuries. He is at work on a new invention. Years ago, before he learned to repair TVs, he worked at a cotton gin. An old man once showed him a trick. The old man attached a piece of wire to the end of a wire brush, then touched the loose end of the wire to the bottom of a light bulb. When the brush was held against a running gin belt, static electricity ran down the wire and made the bulb burn.

Joe believes that if a wheel made of just the right material was lowered from a moving Tradewind travel trailer until the wheel touched the road, and if a contact brush made of just the right material was attached to the top of the wheel to pick up the static, and if the proper means of conveying the static could be devised—there might be just enough electricity to charge the storage battery in the back of the Tradewind. Then the trailer would never have to be near a power source.

If this one works, he intends to hold out for a royalty deal.

Of course, he has no idea what the proper materials are or how to devise the proper means of conveyance. He expects it will take him quite a while to find out.

BORN AGAIN

LELA was sitting on her stool, watching R. V. Eldridge shoot pool, when Sonny walked in. It was the second time she'd seen his face in two days after not seeing it for three months. Yesterday she'd picked up the *Enterprise Tocsin* and there he was on page 1, him and Sheriff Kittle escorting Walter West into the courthouse. Walter and the sheriff were both over six feet tall, and something about their cumulative size and Sonny's lack of it suggested it was Sonny, not Walter, who was headed for a trial.

Sonny said, "Hey, Lela."

"Hi."

R. V. laid down his cue stick. "Hey, Sonny," he said. His voice was loud and thick. He hung around drinking every afternoon now that he'd been laid off at the catfish plant. He had something on his mind besides pool and beer, but Lela pretended not to know it. "Hear you arrested a royal son of a bitch," he said.

"I ain't no genealogist. I don't make judgments about lineage. He's a dope salesman's all I know."

"Folks couldn't believe it. Sonny run Walter in. Heard it everywhere I went."

"Guess that proves your ears work."

"My eyes work too."

"That's miraculous, R. V."

"Tell you what my eyes picked up last weekend." R. V. leaned against the wall and crossed his arms. "Me and Tim Nix was over at the When Club in Leland when Walter strolled in with a little girl he'd filched from a dorm at Delta State. There was a loud band playing the Dire Straits. Evidently Walter's partial to a different kind of music. He handed the guitar player a bill between tunes and ordered him to play 'Whiskey Bent and Hell Bound.' This kid was a little tie-dyed type about your size. He said, 'Sorry, man,' and Walter stiff-armed him backwards off the bandstand. The bouncer came tearing out of the back room, ready to slice meat, but when he saw who'd started the trouble, he just stopped and said, 'Mr. West, I have to ask you to quit that.'"

Sonny said, "That's a nice tale, R. V. You get tired of being unemployed, maybe you can cut a record of stories like Jerry Clower." He mounted a stool, laid a dollar on the bar, and said, "Got any coffee, Lela?"

He told her later that he'd like to come over.

•   •   •

Lela left work at six and went home.

For the past two years she'd lived in the trailer park behind Kelly's Truckstop. The trailer and the park and the truckstop belonged to Beer Smith, the old man who also owned the bar where she worked. She thought of herself as one of his reclamation projects. The guy who sang in the bar every night was a paraplegic who'd been hurt years ago working construction. The manager of the trailer park, a spindly man named Turner, had once owned the park with his brother. One day, when they were working on a jacked-up double-wide, crawling around underneath it, something happened—no one ever knew what, least of all Turner—and the mobile home slid off its support; Turner rolled free, but his brother didn't. Turner's hair turned white in two weeks, he refused to leave his office, all the tenants moved out, and by the time Beer bought the place the weeds were hip-high. Turner did a stint in Whitfield. When they released him, Beer took him on.

Lela herself used to drink way too much and, from time to time, she went crazy. When that happened, she'd dress herself up in skimpy clothes, paint her face with every beauty aid she owned, and when she finally had herself looking like a resident of a science-fiction whorehouse, she'd drive to a truckstop in some place like Winona or Senatobia—it had to be at least forty miles from home, which at the time was Yazoo City—and let the first fellow who showed interest pick her up.

She'd been married once to a long-haul trucker named Lee Starnes. They had their arguments, but he never hit her and to her knowledge he never slept around, so she thought the marriage was a decent one. Then one day he failed to come home. Two weeks later a money order arrived in the mail along with a picture postcard. The description in the upper left-hand corner of the card was blotted out. Beneath it Lee had written, *Guess where?* The envelope containing the card and the money order had been mailed from Winfield, Kansas, but the picture on the card was a street scene from some big city—lots of lights and tall buildings and a movie marquee, advertising something called *Night of the Shooting Stars.* She got a money order and a post-card once a month. Always he crossed out the caption and wrote, *Guess where?*

Sonny's pickup was parked near her trailer. He'd doffed his uniform and was wearing jeans and a white tee shirt. He sat on her steps, looking off across the cotton field; a few hundred yards away, on the other side, the high-school football team was practicing, and you could occasionally hear pads popping, the hoarse curse of a coach.

She walked over and sat down beside him. "What've you been up to?" she said. "Besides busting Walter."

"Nothing much. Actually quite a bit." He studied his palms. His hands were small and smooth, callus-free. She had not known many hands like those.

"Such as what?"

"Well, I made my peace with Evie."

"I figured that."

"I'm back living with her and the kids."

"Figured that too."

"Plus I got baptized."

"That I hadn't figured."

He stood and jammed his hands into his hip pockets. She'd never seen anyone else do that. It signified Sonny was nervous.

He said, "It's not something I set out to do."

"Don't apologize."

"I'm not apologizing. I'm just stating a fact. I don't know hardly anybody I like that goes to church."

She asked him how it happened. He said that one evening he went by the house to take some groceries to Evie. They ended up arguing like always, and like always he demanded a divorce. This time she surprised him, said yes. But she told him he'd first have to go see the new minister out at Fairview.

"Only thing that could make me visit a preacher," he told Lela, "was a chance to get shed of Evie. I called him up and ferried my ass right out there." He said he disliked the preacher immediately, first because he was a preacher but also because he was large and analytic. He commenced to lecture Sonny on God's Law—"You're a lawman," he said at one point, "yet you trample God's statutes"—and after a few minutes of that, Sonny said, "You sound like a damn insurance salesman." He said the preacher turned red, swept papers off his desk, and said, "That's right, you little son of a bitch, I am. And you could use some." He said Sonny reminded him of Barney Fife, he was just a little pest with a badge, and someday somebody mean and abrupt was apt to put a barrel to his belly.

"And you fell for that?" Lela said.

"Not for a day or two." Sonny paced a patch of ground near the steps. "I never told you this, but my uncle used to be the sheriff up in Panola County. Back in the fifties, when it was dry, he made a deal with all the bootleggers. He'd raid them once a month for ten percent of whatever was on hand. One day he headed out in the woods to this old fellow's still, and the guy drilled about sixty holes in him. Last thing in the world I ever wanted to be was a cop, but that's what happened. Brother Watson pushed the right button."

Lela felt tired, and the conversation was tiring her worse. She'd lost men to other women, to the highway, and now to Jesus Christ.

"You've got a wife anyhow," she said. "Kids too. I knew that from the outset. It's good you got saved."

"I didn't set out to," he said.

•　　　•　　　•

Similarity had seeped into her days.

Most mornings she woke groggy from the sleeping pills she took. They were a new brand, her doctor claimed they left no aftereffects, but she knew they did. One morning she walked to Mr. Quik, bought the Memphis paper, went home and ate breakfast, then returned to Mr. Quik to buy the paper again. When the clerk asked if she'd lost the first one, she recalled having bought it; she even thought maybe she'd read it. She forgot phone calls, few and treasured though they were. She stopped taking the pills for a time, but without them she couldn't sleep.

She'd lie around the trailer until lunchtime, reading or watching TV. At noon she went to work. At six she got off. Sometimes in the evenings she'd hang around and drink a beer, but if she had more than one, Beer Smith would glare at her over the bar and venture some nasty remarks. So she'd usually go home, eat

BORN AGAIN • 65
BORN AGAIN • 65

supper, read or watch TV again, take the pills and drop off. It had been like that since the thing with Sonny ended.

One evening, while she was halfway watching a game show, she heard a car pull into her yard. She peeped out the window. It was a yellow MG. The guy at the wheel wore sunglasses. When he got out, she saw that he was dressed to play tennis; the handle of his racket leaned against the passenger door. He pulled off his glasses and walked over to the trailer.

"Hi," he said when she opened the door. "Can I come in?"

"What for?"

He grinned. "I knew you'd ask that," he said. "I'm Wade Watson. I think maybe Sonny mentioned me."

"You're the preacher?"

"If I say yes, does that mean I can't come in?"

"No," she said. "Come on."

He followed her into the living room. She switched off the TV, then stood by the set, not knowing what to do. She gestured at the couch and told him to have a seat.

He sat down and crossed his legs. "Sometimes people wonder," he said, "whether or not they should offer me a beer. If the day's hot and the beer's cold, the answer's yes."

"I don't have any. I've got some Cokes."

She opened one for him, set it on her coffee table, and sat down in her lone armchair.

His eyes roved over her furnishings, then rotated slowly toward the ceiling; they lingered on a water stain. "I grew up in one of these," he said. He told her he'd been raised down close to Belzoni, his father had farmed fish before anyone else, and the family's trailer had stood near the fishpond.

"Right out in the middle of an open field," he said.

"That's not the best place to park one."

"You bet it's not," he said. "My father lived in fear of the elements. Every time the weather bureau issued a tornado watch, he'd make my mother and me crouch in the hallway, on the theory that it was the safest part of the structure. Of course, the whole thing would have blown to Alabama if a tornado had hit it. But he'd put us there, then he'd slip on a pair of hip boots and a yellow raincoat with a rubber hood. He'd grab a big flashlight and a .22 pistol and head outside. I don't know if he aimed to shoot the tornado or what. Once I looked out the window and saw him standing in the yard, staring at the sky, with rain cascading down his face." Watson shook his head. "You can't live in fear of the elements," he said.

She said, "Tornadoes don't worry me much."

"That's good. But something must."

"No, nothing does." When she heard herself say that, she recognized the truth. Nothing worried her. She didn't worry about losing anything, because she owned nothing worth having; she didn't worry about losing anybody, because she had no one who mattered. Loss was all that had ever worried her, and the possibility of it no longer existed.

He said, "I find that hard to believe."

The MG in the yard, the white tennis shorts, the satisfied tilt of his chin—all annoyed her. She said, "If you can't believe it, that's your problem."

He crossed his arms. "I'll tell you what I think worries you," he said. "It's the picture you see when you look at yourself. You're like a disposable diaper. You get used and tossed into the dumpster."

He had chosen the right image: trash was what she felt like, like some old throwaway item. She looked away from him. Her face had grown warm, and there was wetness in her eyes.

He said, "Listen, Lela." His voice sounded softer. "There's a doctor here in town named Danny Harrington. Right after I moved here, my wife found a black bubble on my right shoulder. It always bled after I jogged. She insisted I go to the doctor, and not knowing one from another, I called Danny. He took one look at the thing and said, 'We'll take it off in the morning.' I asked if he thought it was serious, and he said, 'It could be melanoma, and if it is you've got two months to live.'

"Now I believe I know what awaits me after this world, but I've got a wife and two kids, and they're not anxious to see me go. So the week I had to wait for the biopsy was not the most joyful of my life. When the results came in, Danny phoned me and said, 'It's what I thought. A particle got under your skin and crystallized. It's nothing to worry about.'

"When he said that, I said, 'Just stay where you are. I'm on my way to kick your ass.' I drove straight to his office intending to do that.

"After I got there, he told me something I'll never forget. Once he had a young woman come in with a suspicious-looking lump under her right arm. He told her they'd better remove it just to be on the safe side. He scheduled her for the next morning, but she didn't come back till eight months later. By then she had advanced lymph-node cancer. She was dead in six weeks. Danny said that now, as a rule of thumb, he tries to scare the hell out of everybody.

"I look for lumps too," Watson said. "I search for the sores in the spirit. We've all got them. And only one cure will suffice."

He was leaning toward her now, radiating attention.

It warmed her; she soaked in it.

•   •   •

She recalled a standard scene from TV westerns.

A saloon girl straightens out her kinks, washes her face, slips on a gingham dress that hides her ankles, and brazens Sunday worship. When she walks down the aisle, fifty pairs of female eyes bake her back; fifty male faces turn scarlet. Her neck is as stiff as the stock of a shotgun.

It was not like that. No one here knew her but Sonny and Watson. Sonny's eyebrows climbed his forehead when she passed his pew. His wife was flipping through her hymnal.

The song leader, whom Lela thought she recognized from the post office, asked the congregation to stand. He led them through "Standing on the Promises." Then Watson called on Sonny to pray.

Sonny seemed taken by surprise. His hands jumped toward his hip pockets, stopped, dangled loosely in the air, and finally homed on the back of the pew before him. "Dear God," he said. For a long time that was all. She glanced his way: his eyes were clamped shut. "Dear God," he said again. "All I can say's I'm glad we're here. I can't say why I am. I just am. Every single one of us. Amen."

Afterwards, she could not remember Watson's sermon. She remembered Sonny's prayer, and she remembered the little girl who sat beside her. She was five or six, plump and blonde, and she wore a knee-length dress the same shade of red as the center-aisle carpet. Once the sermon had started, she amused herself by playing a trick with her left thumb. She popped it in and out of its joint, again and again, apparently without pain. When she realized Lela was watching her, she grinned and sped up her routine.

Her mother saw her. She leaned over and whispered in the little girl's ear. The little girl quit for several minutes. Then she peeped at Lela, smiled, and did it once more.

Lela was trying to recall the last time she'd been so close to a child for so long. It seemed farther away than childhood itself.

She left aiming not to come back. But on Sundays there was no work, nowhere to go, nothing to do save sit on the trailer steps with Beer and watch the trucks roll in, air brakes sighing. She did her share of sighing too.

She skipped two weeks of church and returned. After the ser-

vice, Watson—whose sermon she'd found surprisingly bland—
seized her hand and said she had to meet his wife.

Alice was an overweight redhead, not the lithe polite blonde
she'd expected. "Hey, Lela," she said. "I'm glad you came
back." She leaned closer and muttered, "Thought maybe the
choir scared you off. It's that woman in the front row with a neck
like a giraffe's. She thinks she's Leontyne Price. It's awful,
isn't it?"

"I didn't really notice it."

"You know, you and I ought to get together. You off on Tuesday evenings?"

She picked Lela up the following Tuesday in the MG. They
drove over to the Marina in Greenville, where they ate some
river catfish. Then they sat outside on the deck drinking coffee.
It was mid-August now, almost time for school. Boatloads of
drunk teenagers skimmed Lake Furguson in what was probably
their final spate of skiing.

Alice said, "I never did that."

"Drink or ski?"

"I drank but I didn't ski. What about you?"

"I did both."

"At once?"

"Sometimes."

"I never skied," Alice said, "because I was so big back in high
school—even bigger than I am now. Once my brother and two of
his friends tried to teach me over on Lake Washington. But they
had a tiny old Wizard outboard on the boat, and it just couldn't
pull me up. They dragged me a quarter of a mile before I let go.
All three of them fell out of the boat giggling."

"It would've pulled you up," Lela said, "if you'd held your legs
right."

"It doesn't *bother* me anymore," Alice said. "I feel real comfortable at my present weight. Besides, Wade won't ever di-

vorce me for being fat because he doesn't believe in divorce."
She sipped her coffee, set the cup down, and said, "He wants to
baptize you bad."

"I guess saving somebody like me's a real accomplishment."

"Honey, it's not accomplishment he believes in. It's the Holy
Ghost."

"The Holy Ghost is hard for me to swallow."

"Me too."

"You?"

"Understand, I don't tell him that. It's not that I disbelieve it
all, it just that severe doubts beset me. But you ought to let him
baptize you anyhow."

"Why?"

"It'd make him feel so good," Alice said and laughed. "Seriously, they're some nice folks at the church. We had a women's
softball team in the spring and summer, and there's powder-puff
football in the fall. We all get together and behave like kids. It's a
great place to meet folks."

Lela didn't want to give in. "I meet folks at work."

"Can you play softball with them?"

Lela said, "They favor other forms of recreation."

Alice laughed so hard she spilled coffee on her lap, and she
laughed so long that Lela finally joined in. They sat and talked
until almost ten o'clock.

Three weeks later Lela made the trek to the altar. Watson
put his arm around her, and several old ladies hugged her. He
scheduled her baptism for the Labor Day weekend, and he gave
her a New American Standard Bible, which she carried home,
laid atop the TV, and never opened.

·　　　·　　　·

She spent the week before her baptism looking for a new job.
She applied at Modern and Ludlow, the two small factories in
town, as well as at each grocery store, the Pizza Hut, McDon-

ald's. Women's clothing stores she ruled out: clerks there tended toward primness, which no amount of rebirthing could invest in her. She was looking forward to the powder-puff games, dinner on the grounds, cottage prayer. Decent company, in other words, and she'd claim faith in Jesus or Richard Nixon to get it.

Somebody alerted Beer Smith. Thursday evening he stomped into the bar, beating field dust from his khakis. He heaved himself onto a stool. It was a quarter before six; the bar was empty but for them.

"Well," he said, "I hear you're searching for work."

"I was going to tell you."

"Looks like you told everybody else first."

"I'm sorry, Beer."

"You want more money? Why didn't you ask?"

"It's not more money."

"You want less money? What is it?"

"I don't want to work in a bar."

"R. V.'s been pawing you, hasn't he? I got a boot was designed for his butt."

"You're not my uncle, Beer."

His face, which had been red when he came in, lost about two-thirds of its color. "That's the second time you told me that," he said. "Remember the first?"

It was two years ago at the truckstop. She'd gone there three or four nights in a row. Right across the highway stood a run-down motel, a place where ragweed reigned in the parking lot and half the bulbs on the sign were burned out, and Beer had seen her cross the road with men too many nights running. He'd sat down beside her at the counter and said, "We don't often see your kind here. Sure adds color to the place." She was so drunk she could barely see his face. He said, "Didn't you wander off from the French Quarter?"

Her tongue had melded with her palate. "Sorry," she slurred.

"You ought to be. But it's yourself that deserves an apology."

"You're not my uncle."

"If I was," he told her, "your momma and me would goddam hold us a summit." He walked behind the counter, filled a Styrofoam cup with coffee, then gripped her arm and led her out. Soon she was sitting on his porch swing with half a quart of coffee in her belly. Sobriety returned in a flood. She always cried when that happened.

He watched her for a minute. Then he said, "You're not a pro, are you?"

"At some things."

"Like what?"

"Disgusting myself."

"Ain't nobody'll pay you for that. You got a job somewhere?"

She'd been working part time at her brother's grocery store in Yazoo City. Otherwise she lived off the money orders Lee mailed her. She said, "Not really."

"You want one?"

She knew she needed a change, and she was ready to try anything anybody suggested. She could think of no solutions for herself. She said, "I guess so."

Beer drove her to Yazoo City the next day, loaded her stuff in his pickup, and moved her into her trailer. She went to work tending bar. For a few days she thought he might expect her to tend to something else too. Then one evening, when they were sitting on her steps watching the sun go down, he said, "You act like you're expecting me to grab you any minute."

"Don't be mad at me," she said, "but the thought did enter my mind."

He said, "Ten years ago my daughter got shot in the head in a poolroom over in Little Rock. Her and her husband were in there together, and whoever killed her was riding by in a pickup. It was a Saturday night, and whoever it was just fired one shot in there at random, just for the hell of it, and nobody ever caught him.

"A month after that I came home one evening and found my wife cold on the couch. She'd had a heart attack. The TV was on, and I always wondered if she didn't die watching the evening news. I'll never forget one thing. There was half a glass of orange juice on the coffee table. I don't know why I remember that, but I do." He pulled out a cigarette, lit it, and said, "I don't grab women, not no more, so rest easy."

Now, staring at him across the bar, she could see how much she'd hurt him by looking for work. But too much of what she did in life she did to avoid disappointing someone. The someone was rarely her. The someones were the Sonnys, the Watsons, the Beer Smiths, the nameless many she'd known. All they had to do was make eye contact, spend some words on her, act concerned. She would rather have been a woman like Alice: secure in her unlovely bulk, at home in a house, surrounded by her kids and a man dispossessed of the impulse to stray.

She said, "Beer, I'm going to church now. I got saved."

"From what?"

"I'm not sure."

His face turned red again. When he leaned over the bar, she could feel the heat from his breath. "You know what a person needs saving from?" he said. "Growing old. Getting cancer. Getting shot at the post office by some guy you've said good morning to for years. Having your throat slit by a stranger while you sleep."

His breath grew even hotter. He went on and on, piling up the phrases, constructing a list of diseases and disasters. She let the words wash over her. In her mind she was making a list of her own.

It differed fundamentally from his.

•   •   •

A large square of poster paper hung on the wall behind Watson's desk. It was sectioned into blocks, one block for each Sunday of the year. Many of the blocks contained numbers, mostly 1s and 2s, though occasionally there would be a 3, and once there was a 5. He pointed at the Sunday before Labor Day, where he'd already entered a 1 for her.

It was Saturday afternoon, and they'd met to rehearse the baptism. He asked her to stand before his desk. He put one hand behind her shoulders. "When I lean you backwards," he said, "don't move your feet—if you do, we'll both end up at the bottom of the tank. Just trust me to support you. I'll press a handkerchief over your nose to keep the water out." They practiced several times and he told her she could go.

Sunday morning, near the end of the worship service, she and Alice rose together and entered the dressing room behind the baptistry. Alice, holding a towel over her forearm, watched her undress. When Lela pulled out the dress she intended to wear, Alice said, "The skirt's too full, Lela. It's going to ride up over your hips when the water gets under it." She laid the towel down, rummaged through her purse until she found some safety pins, then bound the skirt tightly to Lela's hips and legs.

Watson waited at the top of the baptistry steps. He was wearing a different suit now and a pair of athletic socks. He whispered, "I'll open the door for you when I'm ready." The wooden stairs squeaked beneath his feet. She heard water slosh. He opened the door and disappeared.

The baptistry was a glass-fronted tank one level higher than the choir loft. When the red velvet curtains were drawn open, the congregation could see everything above the participants' knees. Waiting at the top of the steps, she heard Watson in there addressing the congregation, but she could not make out his words. Soon the door opened a crack. She walked down the steps into the water.

It was lukewarm, level with her waist. She stepped into the tank. A bright light blinded her. When her eyes had adjusted, she looked out into the sanctuary. Sonny was sitting in the third row from the front. She thought she saw him nod.

Watson's lips were moving. He raised a Bible, waved it at the congregation, then laid it on the railing. He pulled a handkerchief from his pocket, placed his hand on her back, and leaned her backwards.

She saw him hovering over her, the white handkerchief descending, covering her face, shutting out light, and as the water rolled over her, she reached up and gripped his arm and held on.

FAMILY MEN

UNCLE CECIL knew the birthday of every church organist in Tupelo, Mississippi, and once a year, using his patrolmen as delivery boys, he dispatched each of the ladies a dozen red roses. But the last time he set foot in a church was in 1952, when Grandma Campbell died. He didn't attend Grandpa Campbell's funeral in 1955. Grandpa Campbell had requested that his funeral be held in the shop at Delta Implement Company, where he had worked on tractors and officiated at fish fries for twenty-five years; his two younger children, Dad and Aunt Mary, didn't take the request seriously, but Uncle Cecil did. The funeral was held at Fairview Baptist Church. Uncle Cecil staged a personal boycott. Later, he showed up at graveside, listened to the preacher say words over the coffin, then climbed into his car and drove back to Tupelo, 175 miles away.

And Dad didn't see him again for thirteen years.

But he heard from him. Each Christmas Eve at eleven o'clock Uncle Cecil would phone. The year I was eleven—I can date it exactly; it was the year I received my Fender Coronado—he asked to speak to me.

I was always up late on Christmas Eve because we opened our presents then. Dad handed me the phone. Even though I had never heard Uncle Cecil speak before, I knew immediately that something was wrong with his voice. He sounded as if his mouth were full of peanut butter. "How about," he said, "a little 'Faded Love'?"

It's important to know that I was musically precocious. At age nine I appeared on "The Big Six," a country-music program on WABT in Greenwood. I was playing a Sears acoustic back then. I sang "Cold Cold Heart."

I covered the mouthpiece with my palm and said to Dad: "He wants me to do 'Faded Love.' His voice sounds funny. He's drunk, isn't he?"

Dad's jaw trembled. "Shut up," he said. "Just sing 'Faded Love' and then give me the phone."

I plugged in my new Fender and sang.

When I finished, Uncle Cecil said, "That's pretty."

•   •   •

Christmas Eve of the following year he failed to call. My father phoned the next morning to see if anything was wrong. Afterwards, I heard him tell Mother that Aunt Dottie said Uncle Cecil had "quit."

That night, Dad said, "I think we better go see him next weekend." He called again to make sure it was all right. Uncle Cecil said for me to bring my guitar.

Though I had never seen my uncle in person, I remembered having once been shown a picture of him. The picture was in the brown photo album that rested on the top shelf of my dad's closet, which was always kept locked. I asked Dad to show me the picture again.

The man in the black-and-white snapshot looked almost exactly like Dad, except for his hair and eyebrows, which seemed darker than my father's. He had the same square chin, the long sloping jaw. He wore a greyish-looking coat, with a darker-colored strap cutting diagonally across his chest. Right over his heart there was a silver badge, shaped like the state of Missis-

sippi. "He was a highway bull for nine years," Dad said. "A boot-
legger shot him in the back in 1951. He quit and joined the Tupelo
police force after that."

When Dad stood up to put the album back in the closet, a
loose photo dropped out. He bent and scooped it off the floor,
but not before I got a good look at it. It was a picture of him. He
wore a sailor's uniform. Two other sailors had their arms around
his shoulders. On a table in front of them stood several tall
bottles. Dad looked strangely young in the photo. He had a silly
grin on his face.

In bed that night I thought about the grin and felt troubled.

•   •   •

We got to Tupelo late Saturday afternoon. Aunt Dottie, who was
short and lumpy and wore black-rimmed glasses, opened the
door. She hugged everybody. When she got to me she went
right ahead and said, "Lord how you've grown," even though she
had never seen me be any other size. "Y'all come on in," she
said. "Cecil's on duty right now, but he'll be home around six."

We sat down in the living room. "Did Josephine and them
make it this year?" Mother asked.

"No. Myrtle, would you believe we haven't seen that girl in
three years? But Baltimore's a long ways off. They just haven't
been able to get down here. There's a table of stuff in there that
her and Jimmy sent, though. Cheese and canned hams and I
don't know what all. Oh, and let me show you something we got
from them back in the summer."

Aunt Dottie picked up a picture postcard off the coffee table
and handed it to Mother.

"Ain't that a big one?"

"Oh, Lord."

"Let's see," said Dad.

I looked over his shoulder at the postcard. It was a picture of an Eskimo woman kneeling before a giant cabbage. The cabbage came up to the woman's chin.

Dad flipped the card over. The note in the upper left-hand corner said that cabbages grown in Alaska sometimes weighed as much as fifty pounds.

"That'd go a ways, wouldn't it?"

"I guess so," Dad said, laying the card down. "How's Cecil, Dottie?"

"Well, Mutt, you know his eyesight's been going bad now for several years. I don't know if he told you the other day when you called, but they put him in R and I—that's Records and Identification—last year. He don't much like sitting at a desk. But he's sure been behaving lots better since the doctor scared him last summer. I guess all in all he's a different man completely."

Aunt Dottie said there were some records I could play in the bedroom, so while she talked to Mother and Dad, I went back there. Uncle Cecil had more records than I had ever seen before. Hundreds of them. Hank Williams, Bob Wills, Patsy Cline, Johnny Horton, Bill Monroe and the Blue Grass Boys. I played several albums I hadn't heard. Then I fell asleep on the bed. When I woke up, it was dark. I got up and wandered back into the living room. I was just in time to see Uncle Cecil walk into the house.

Dad stood up. "Hi, there, old law dog," he said. He shook Uncle Cecil's hand.

Uncle Cecil squinted at Dad through a pair of thick lenses. He smiled. "Had a harder time rediscovering Tupelo than Columbus had finding America, didn't you?" he said. "Took you thirteen years."

"Well, you know how us Campbell men are."

"I do. I expect you'll puzzle it out yourself just any year now."

Uncle Cecil hugged Mother then squinted just past her at me. "That yonder must be the music man," he said.

Dumbly, I let him squeeze my paw.

"I'll go get washed up," he said and left the room.

When I was sure he couldn't hear, I whispered, "Is that him?"

"That's the old law dog."

He didn't look at all like the man in the photo album. He looked like the President, like Lyndon Baines Johnson, LBJ, and I intended to bring it to everyone's attention. "He looks," I said, "just exactly like LBJ."

Dad looked at me and slowly shook his head. "I wouldn't tell him that," he said.

•　　　•　　　•

Aunt Dottie had fried a chicken, and there were green beans, potato salad, and pecan pie. I stuffed myself. I knew I was getting to be a fat kid, but I didn't care. Eating made me happy.

After supper, Uncle Cecil said, "Let's have some picking."

Dad went out to the car and got my guitar and my amp. At that time I was playing in a four-piece country band with the head of the Soil Conservation Service in my hometown, a local high-school football coach, and an attendant at Gresham's Amoco. But I had recently discovered I liked the Rolling Stones, as well as Janis Joplin and the Grateful Dead and the Who, and the previous week Dad had caught me standing before a mirror, twisting my hips, making faces, and whacking the holy hell out of my Fender while I bawled a verse of "Satisfaction." Now, to forestall a lapse into R & B or worse, Dad said, "Play 'Rock of Ages' for Uncle Cecil."

I knew it would do no good to protest, so I put on my thumbpick and plucked my way through the hymn, tickling the small strings with my pinky in the style of Chester A. As soon as I finished, Uncle Cecil said, "Lord God, that was beautiful. Now play 'Honky Tonkin'.'"

I picked up my flatpick and made the old Hank Williams tune

sound like something Keith Richards might have written. Uncle Cecil and I patted our feet together. Dad frowned at both of us.

I played five or six more bouncy numbers, slipping in a Richardsesque rendition of "Johnny B. Goode." Finally, Dad leaned over and switched off my amp. "You've entertained the folks plenty," he said.

"I could listen to him pick all night," Uncle Cecil said. He asked me if I'd like to see the jail.

I said sure, so we piled into our car, Dad and Uncle Cecil and I, and drove downtown. Uncle Cecil showed me the Records Division, where he worked; he showed me the drunk tank, the juvenile detention cell, and a vault where firearms were kept.

On the way back home, he said, "Mutt, let's stop off at the store."

"What for?"

"What do you mean, what for? Can't I go to the store if I want to?"

Dad laughed, but I thought he sounded nervous. "Boy, you don't need nothing from no store," he said. "Your old belly's plenty full."

"Stop the goddam car."

"I don't think so."

"Stop it, goddammit."

"Cecil," Dad said, "my son's in the car."

"Well, stop the son of a bitch, and I'll get out and you and him can have it. Stop it, Mutt, or I'll just open the goddam door and jump."

Dad slowed to a stop at the corner. We were in a residential section of town. Uncle Cecil opened the door and got out. "I thank you for the ride, brother," he said. "You go on back to the house now and hum hymn songs."

He slammed the car door and ambled off down the sidewalk.

•   •   •

When we got back to the house, my cousin Claude and his wife, Nancy, and their baby were there. Claude is Aunt Mary's son; he and Nancy lived in Oxford, which is about an hour from Tupelo.

Aunt Dottie asked Dad where Uncle Cecil was.

"He went for a walk," Dad said. "Dottie, can I talk to you in the kitchen a minute?"

They were gone for five or ten minutes. After they came back, we sat around listening to Claude talk about how he was doing in law school at Ole Miss.

Uncle Cecil came back around ten o'clock, just as Claude and Nancy were about to leave. "Y'all sit back down," he said.

"Well, for just a minute."

Uncle Cecil sat down on the couch between Nancy and me. He pulled off his glasses, rubbed his eyes, and stretched. "Family men," he said. "Me and Mutt and Claude."

I caught a whiff of his breath. It was sweet, minty. "What about me?" I said. "I'll be a family man too."

"Let's hope not," he said. "You pick that guitar too fine."

The baby was lying asleep in Nancy's lap. Suddenly, Uncle Cecil leaned toward the baby, studying it closely. "When was the last time I saw this baby?" he asked.

"October," Nancy said. "Why?"

"It's shrunk."

Dad jumped up out of his chair. "Cecil," he said, "get up and come on outside."

Uncle Cecil looked at me and smiled. "When I get back," he said, "you and me's gonna sing 'Kaw-Liga.'"

But we didn't. We didn't sing "Kaw-Liga." Uncle Cecil and I never got to do the one about the wooden Indian. Dad came back into the house a few minutes later and told Mother and me to get our coats.

Uncle Cecil was right behind him. "Hell yes," he said. "Get your goddam coats. It's fifty degrees. You don't want to freeze."

"Cecil—" Aunt Dottie began.

He leveled his finger at her. "You know what to do," he said, "so do it, Dottie, right quick."

She shut up. Completely.

Mother and Dad and Nancy and Claude and the incredible shrinking baby and I left together.

•   •   •

That was a long time ago. Uncle Cecil has been dead fourteen years. He died less than six months after the only time I saw him. I didn't know him well enough to miss him much. But here's why I'm telling this story.

When we got back from Tupelo that Sunday morning, it was after five o'clock. We had suffered a blowout on the way back; our spare tire was flat, so Dad had been forced to walk five miles to a truckstop for help. We all fell into bed just as soon as we got home.

Around twelve-thirty Mr. Colter Lucas knocked on the door. Mr. Lucas was one of Dad's fellow deacons at Fairview Baptist. I wasn't privy to the conversation that took place, but Mother has told me about it again and again. In fact, for several years now I've been unable to see her without her bringing it up.

Mr. Colter Lucas was on our party line. Whenever our phone rang, he heard it. He told Dad that around 3 A.M. he had grown tired of hearing our phone ring.

Mr. Colter Lucas said maybe Dad needed to learn a thing or two about family responsibility. He said he had a brother in Little Rock himself, and he didn't think his brother was a very good man—he all but knew he played poker for money—but his brother, he said, was still his brother. He said maybe Dad ought to chew on that awhile.

Then he said that on top of everything else, Dad and his family had missed church this morning.

Mr. Colter Lucas said he was only being critical because he loved Dad. Don't forget, he said, you and me are brothers too.

Dad has never been back to church. He sent a letter to the preacher the following week, advising him that he was resigning from the board of deacons.

He made me attend church with Mother until I entered high school. When I stopped going then, he never said a word. I quit the country combo. I formed a rock band, and we played a hybrid kind of stomp, part Allmans, part Creedence, part Stones. I let my hair grow long and stringy, and when George and Tammy played a concert in my hometown, I was out in the cotton field, smoking dope with the wife of the very coach I once picked with. Coach himself was at the concert.

Dad didn't start drinking until I went away to college. Even now he won't drink in my presence. I live in Memphis, which isn't too far from home, and I try to go and see him and Mother every couple of months; when I'm there, he does his drinking in the laundry room, squatting down in the corner behind the washing machine. Sometimes when he's in there I hear him singing. Most of the numbers I recognize as old Baptist hymns.

What bothers me isn't his drinking.

What bothers me, just a little bit, is that he feels like singing and I don't. Music just doesn't move me anymore. I started getting tired of it right after high school.

The last time I even touched a guitar was over three years ago, when I had just started dental school here in Memphis. I kicked around town with a halfway country band, but I only did it because I needed the money.

I met my future wife during a Thursday night gig at Hernando's Hideaway. She says that when she first set eyes on me we were playing "Coward of the County."

She says I was just standing up there on the bandstand, looking as if I didn't quite know where I was.

BETWEEN NOW AND THEN

O<small>N</small> the screen the Greenwood tailback crouched.

"Look," Larkin said. "See how far back his right foot is? Ten to one he totes the mail."

In slow motion the quarterback spun and handed the ball to the tailback, who broke outside, off the tight end and the tackle's double-team.

Larkin said, "Is he coming back?"

Bill Mason, the head coach, said, "Yep."

"Good."

"It won't matter," Mason said. "You can just about bet they won't be in the I. Dantone always tries to surprise you in the opener."

Mason shut off the projector, then removed his wire-rims and rubbed his eyes. Lately, Larkin had noticed, Mason's eyes always looked red. Maybe he'd started drinking. If so, Larkin hoped none of the players caught him buying alcohol. That would set one hell of an example.

Mason folded the glasses and stuck them in his shirt pocket. He said, "I want to go ahead and tell you this before I tell anybody else. This'll be my last year here."

"What?"

"Time to quit."

"Quit coaching?"

"Yep."

"What do you plan to do?"

Mason said, "Guess."

"I don't know."

"What do failed coaches usually do?"

"Sell insurance."

"Interested in a comprehensive health policy?"

"My God, Bill—it'll kill you."

"No, it won't," Mason said, but he didn't sound as if he believed it. He stood, hitched up his khakis, and flipped on the light switch. "I've got children, and children get big and go to college. I just don't make enough here, Jackie. All along I've hoped I'd get the chance to coach college ball, but I'm thirty-eight now, and there's no use fooling myself anymore. This is as far as I go."

Larkin trained his eyes on a stack of shoulder pads in the corner. Mason had made him uncomfortable. He did not like man-to-man talks. The few he had ever had were with his father, and they were one-way affairs in which his father did all the talking and he did all the listening. They had occurred five or six years ago, near the end of his father's life, and he remembered them with embarrassment. His father had confessed that he slept around on Larkin's mother, that often on Sundays he drank before delivering his sermons, and that any day of the week he would rather fish than preach.

It troubled Larkin to see that Mason, a man he respected, had mapped his life out so badly. Just yesterday Larkin had told his players, "In 1979, I'll be thirty. Sometime between now and then, I'll decide whether I want to be the best strength coach on the planet or the best defensive coordinator on the planet, and once I've made up my mind, dying's all that'll halt me."

Now he made himself face Mason and say, "Well, I guess you have to do what you have to do."

"Everybody does."

•　　　•　　　•

After practice Larkin changed clothes and drove home.

Until July he had occupied room 5 at the Delta Vista Motel. Three or four times a year his mother would drive up from Jackson and clean his room and wash his dirty clothes, which he usually shoved under his bed or tossed into the back seat of his VW. But during the summer a Pakistani family had bought the motel, and since they refused to rent by the month, he had taken a room in Emily Turner's house.

Emily was in her late twenties, a small woman with blonde hair and powder-blue eyes. Her ex-husband, Burt, owned the local Pontiac dealership, billed himself "Trader Burt" in TV ads, and spent his weekends piloting a peppermint-candy-striped hot-air balloon, which last year he had landed near midfield during the fourth quarter of the State–Ole Miss game. Mason said his current girlfriend was an MDJC sophomore.

Larkin's arrangement with Emily included breakfast and supper. He liked her cooking but had just about decided the arrangement contained one flaw: her kids were always present at mealtime. Her daughter didn't bother him too much, but her eight-year-old son tormented him. Every night the kid quizzed him nonstop and then found fault with Larkin's answers.

Tonight Richard said, "How come Tubby Ethridge and Phil Fratesi and James Hill all stand up?"

Larkin heaped mashed potatoes on his plate. "So they can read the backs and get to the ball fast."

"So how come Bubba Bowen and Lee Harper don't stand up?"

"They're tackles."

"That's a dumb reason."

Larkin glanced at Emily. She was listening to Margaret talk about a snake some kid had brought to class in a tow sack. He leaned toward Richard. "Richard," he whispered, "just between you and me, you better hope I'm coaching the Dallas Cowboys by the time you get to high school."

Richard said, "You won't be."

"Richard," Emily said, "let Jackie eat."

Larkin smiled to show her she'd lessened life's worries by one hundred percent. As always, she failed to notice him.

That evening, when he stepped out of the shower, he found both children standing in the bathroom gawking at him. They shrieked, "Jackie!" and ran. On the way to his room he heard Emily downstairs berating them.

"You mustn't ever do that again," she said. "Besides. There's nothing funny about the way a man's made."

•   •   •

When he came to work at Indianola, Larkin had convinced Mason weight training was essential. That first year, they bought a Universal Gladiator and two thousand dollars' worth of free weights, and every night for three months they worked on the weight room, painting the walls the school colors, installing foam-rubber padding, and assembling the Universal and a squat rack. This season Larkin expected the work to pay off.

Friday night, Greenwood lined up in the wishbone. On the sideline he watched them shred his defense. They led at the half 21–13.

Jogging to the locker room, Mason said, "Be strategic, Jackie." His breeziness angered Larkin. No wonder the man had not advanced.

Inside, Larkin seized chalk, Xed and Oed the board. "When they run the triple option," he said, "we'll use prearranged stunts. We'll call them *A, B,* and *C.* In *A,* the tackles *tackle* the fullback—don't worry about whether he's got the ball, just put him on the ground. Ends flatten the quarterback. Onside line-backers and corners have pitch." He explained each of the stunts twice, then laid down the chalk and stared at the players until they all got nervous and quit drinking Gatorade. "Right now," he said, "we couldn't face our Maker. Let's get back out and mince ass."

Greenwood graced the end zone no more. Indianola won 30–21.

Usually, Larkin went to Spicey Lott's Burgers after a game and ate the meal he'd been too nervous to eat before the game. Tonight, however, he drove straight home. He'd stopped at Spicey's yesterday for a chocolate shake and before leaving had forecast a shutout.

When he walked into the house, he found Emily relaxing in the living room. She was sitting on the couch, watching Johnny Carson, her bare feet drawn up beneath her. She wore a pink gown with MOMMA stenciled on the front in white letters, and she held a tall glass in her hand. Larkin spied a lime wedge float-ing in the glass.

"Hi, Jackie," she said. "Did you win?"

"Just barely."

"How many points?"

"Nine."

"That's not so little. How about a drink to celebrate?"

This was the first time she'd suggested they socialize. Back when she rented him the room, she'd been downright rude. "I don't want a stranger moving in with me," she'd said. "Unfor-tunately, I need your money." She worked at Seymour Library, lived in the house her father had left her, and according to Mason, refused to accept alimony from Trader Burt.

With approval, Larkin noted now that her toenails were un-painted. He hated painted toenails. "Sure," he said.

"What'll you have?"

"Gin and tonic—but make it weak."

"Weak?"

His cheeks heated up. He said, "I'm always preaching to my players about taking care of their bodies, and I like to practice what I preach."

She said, "Bodies *do* need taking care of." She slipped on her house shoes, picked up her glass, and carried it into the kitchen.

She returned with a fresh drink for herself and another one for Larkin, who had sat down on the couch. She kicked off the house shoes and joined him.

"You got off to a good start," she said. "Cheers."

They raised their glasses.

"I hope you have a good season," she said. "Especially since it's Bill's last."

"You heard about his plans?"

"Burt told me."

"Hard for me to understand—he's won two conference championships, and we've got a strong team this year. We might win the state."

"He has family responsibilities," she said. "Speaking of families, Richard'll probably bombard you with football questions the second he lays eyes on you. I hope you won't mind."

Larkin said, "What a great kid."

"He and Margaret went with Burt to the ball game. It's Burt's night off from his girlfriend. She spends Fridays at her dorm."

Larkin stared intently at the TV: David Frye stood onstage impersonating Nixon. Larkin said, "That's no laughing matter."

"You're telling me."

"I meant the TV. Watergate."

"Oh," she said. "Well, I think Watergate's funny as hell."

"What's funny about it?"

"The sight of several bastards in free fall."

Larkin envisioned Nixon frozen in midair. "When you put it that way," he said, "I guess it is funny."

She didn't reply, so Larkin sipped his drink and after a while began thinking about his next opponent. Belzoni's coach always tried whatever gadget plays he had seen on TV over the weekend; Larkin would spend tomorrow and Sunday with Mason, glued to the set. He looked at the wall clock, saw that it was eleven-thirty, and decided to say goodnight.

Suddenly Emily shifted position. Larkin's sharp peripheral vision, which in college had made him impossible to crack back on, now alerted him to the square inch of bare breast visible between the buttons of Emily's nightgown. She sat there unaware, drinking occasionally, the ice cubes tinkling in her glass. Once or twice she stifled a yawn.

Toward midnight Larkin moved closer.

•   •   •

"It's a good thing our arrangement includes meals," Emily said. She put on a white terry-cloth robe and walked over to her dresser.

Larkin lay in bed watching her. "How come?"

She was brushing her hair. "Because," she said, "if our arrangement didn't include meals and I offered to cook breakfast for you, you might get scared."

Larkin knew what she meant. "I don't know what you mean," he said.

She turned, walked to the bed and, bending, pecked his lips. "I bet you do," she said. "I'm going to cook breakfast. Join me if you want to."

When she left, Larkin closed his eyes and tugged the covers up under his chin. He inhaled the smells of the room, the odor of hair spray, perfume. He had always liked lying in a woman's bed, but he did not like those things that tended to occur when you got up and put on your clothes. His last girlfriend, whom he'd met in Jackson at an MEA conference, lived in Laurel, and though she understood why he could not visit on weekends during the fall, she did not understand why he could not visit during winter and spring. He said attending coaching clinics helped him stay a step ahead of the pack. She said, "You're *several* steps ahead of me." She had broken off the relationship a year ago last summer. When Mason asked if he still saw her, Larkin said, "She wasn't what I thought."

He climbed out of bed now and gathered his clothes. His Jockey shorts dangled from a lamp in the corner.

In the dining room, he found Emily seated at one end of the long oak table. She was crunching a piece of toast and reading the Jackson *Daily News*. Larkin's plate, his silverware, and his coffee cup had been arranged at the other end of the table.

He said, "Did you ever notice how long this table is?"

She looked up from her paper. "Eighty-one and three-quarter inches," she said and resumed reading.

Larkin said, "Let's see . . . that's seven inches longer than me."

"Is it."

"Maybe I ought to move down there."

"If you want to."

Larkin ferried his breakfast to Richard's usual place and sat down. The paper hid Emily's face. He said, "You know, I just don't like the way Gerald Ford looks."

She lowered the paper, flipped it over, and studied the front-page photo. "Now that you mention it," she said, "he does look a little bit stiff."

"Are you a Democrat or a Republican?"

"I'm unaligned," she said. "Completely."

Larkin laughed and so did she. He felt free to eat.

When he finished, it was almost eleven. He'd promised to meet Mason at twelve, but before that he had to drive to the bus station and send a film to the coach in Grenada. He said, "What are you up to today?"

She laid the knives and forks on his plate and stacked it on hers. "I'm up to nothing now," she said. "But Burt'll bring the kids home at four, so I'll be tied up after that."

Larkin would be busy with Mason until five-thirty or six. He said, "Couldn't you get a baby-sitter? I thought we might drive over to Greenville tonight and eat supper."

"What made you think that?"

Larkin said, "Emily, are you playing hard to get?"

"You already got me. Remember? You slid across the couch and whispered in my ear and I whispered in your ear, and after we'd whispered for a while, we kissed, and then you stuck your hand in my shirt and I—"

"What *is* it with you?"

"It's nothing with me." She stood and picked up the dishes. "I could get a baby-sitter, but I'm not going to because I promised to take the kids to see a movie this evening. On Saturdays I put them to bed at ten-thirty. After that, I'll be sitting in the living room reading a book or watching TV. You're welcome to come sit with me. In fact, I wish you would."

That afternoon, watching Georgia Tech play Clemson, Larkin told Mason, "I hate trick plays. If I had my way, I'd outlaw traps and reverses and flea-flickers—anything sneaky."

Mason said, "Then you'd have to outlaw sneaky defense."

•   •   •

Larkin happened into the living room at ten-thirty. When Emily felt the kids were asleep, they went to his room and made love. Afterwards, she propped herself up in bed and surveyed the scene. Larkin watched her eyes rove over his scattered clothes, the piles of ungraded drivers'-ed quizzes, the waist-high stacks of *Sport* and *Sports Illustrated*. Wadded scraps of paper littered the room.

She pointed at the wall beside the bed and said, "What's this?"

Larkin, leaning over, saw the rows of Xs and Os. "I ran out of paper," he said, "I meant to erase it."

"I hear you're a fine coach."

"I still have some things to learn."

"You think they might offer you Bill's job?"

He already knew Mason planned to recommend him. But he'd hatched plans of his own. In the last year, he'd become friends with Lou Higgins, the defensive coordinator at Tennessee. Higgins had told him Tennessee would need a defensive-end coach next year, and he'd said that if Larkin's defense played well this season, he could probably persuade Bill Battle to give him a job. Larkin planned to ship Higgins all his game films.

Larkin said, "I guess they might offer it to me. I'm not counting on it."

"I hope they do. If that's what you want." She pushed back the covers and slid out of bed.

"Leaving?"

"I have to." She dressed, cracked his door and peeked out, then whispered good-night.

He stayed away the next couple of nights, but then he began going to the living room most evenings. Emily was usually reading, but she closed her book when he sat down.

"How was your day?"

"Fine. How was yours?"

"Fine."

They'd sit a while in silence, until he cleared his throat and said, "Want to go upstairs?"

In bed her body strained against his. She whispered his name, clutched his hips, and pulled him deeper. He detected need and warned himself to watch out. After they made love, she disarmed him. She asked if he always gnawed a woman's earlobe when he came. Pointing at his stockinged feet, she claimed sex minus socks was beyond him. He said, "Baloney," shed the socks, and to his amazement failed to achieve an erection.

She said, "Samson's hair. Larkin's Gold Cups."

During the day, he saw her only at breakfast. Though the library was two blocks from the school, she never asked him to eat lunch with her. She never suggested they go shopping. At first, he found the lack of demands puzzling. But after a while he thought he understood. He'd lived in Indianola four years, and though Emily had been divorced for much of that time, he'd never seen her in a restaurant, in a store, or on the street with a man. Aside from Trader Burt, a few truck drivers who pulled long hauls for Lewis Grocery Company, and four or five chronic drunks who more or less lived at the Beer Smith Lounge, every guy in town over twenty-five was attached. Except Larkin.

He knew a tactical advantage when he saw one. But as the weeks passed and he continued seeing Emily, he felt an urge to relinquish the edge.

One night in bed he said, "We're seeing a lot of each other."

She said, "That's because we keep taking our clothes off."

"Be serious. We see each other every night, but I know next to nothing about you."

She rolled over and propped her chin on his chest. Her blue eyes were inches from his. She said, "What do you want to know?"

Larkin heard himself say, "Everything."

She told him she had grown up in Indianola and gone to college at Ole Miss, where she married Burt when she was twenty. The next year, after graduation, she gave birth to Margaret. Richard was born fifteen months later, the same day Burt flunked out of law school.

Larkin knew Burt as the nuisance who showed up at Legion Field wearing black nylon coaching pants, an old-gold turtleneck, and a black-and-gold IHS cap. He and the kids sat right behind the bench. In critical moments he hollered at Mason. "Bill. Hey, Bill. Run Sam Tiery on the double reverse."

Lately every time Burt yelled, Larkin thought of Emily. That disturbed him. His mind belonged in the game.

He said, "So Burt studied law."

"He wanted to be a politician. Back in '68, he ran for the state legislature. He thought he could win if he appealed to the working-man, so he bought a hard hat and rented a bulldozer and had a TV commercial filmed with him driving the machine. He liked the ad so much he trucked the bulldozer to rallies on a flatbed. He'd drive it around a vacant lot, push over a few bushes, and get his picture in the paper. The thing was, he didn't really know how to handle a bulldozer. He lost control of it in Morehead. Plowed down a row of parking meters, ran over a VW, tore up the pavement, and smashed into the pool hall. He spent five times more than any other candidate and finished dead last in the primary—got fewer than three hundred votes. He started sleep-ing around after that. At least I don't think he did it before."

"What attracted you to him?"

"His seriousness."

When he laughed, she said, "I mean it. He was four years older than I was, and he used to lie in bed puffing on a cigarette and telling me all he hoped to accomplish. None of it quite panned out. He's a small-town businessman who runs after young girls. But I'll tell you one thing. He can fly the hell out of that balloon. Land it on a penny."

With his thumbs, he parted her bangs. He said, "Emily, why do you stay in Indianola?"

"I like the night life."

"Come on."

"Okay—it's because I don't want to move the kids away from Burt."

"He left you."

"I know, but I just couldn't move them away. Not under any circumstances. He's still their father."

"So you put your own life on hold. For how long? Ten years?"

She sat up. The covers rolled off her shoulders. She clamped her fingers around his wrist and pulled his hand to her breast. "I'm living," she said. "Feel my heartbeat? I eat, I sleep, and I breathe."

He felt her pulse beneath his palm. Wetting his lips, he observed, "Of course, there's me. You've got me."

When he woke the next morning, he wished he had not said that. But Emily behaved no differently that evening or any other evening, so he concluded he'd done himself no damage.

•　　　　•　　　　•

The defense recorded four straight shutouts after the opener and would have registered a fifth if the offense hadn't turned the ball over on the three against Leland. In the remaining four games they gave up six, three, seven, and three points. The team finished ten and zero. After the last regular-season game, the superintendent told Larkin unofficially that the school board would offer him Mason's job. Larkin said, "Great," and left it at that.

The state play-offs began the week before Thanksgiving. Indianola drew Bay St. Louis and lost a coin toss determining the home field. Mason moaned about that, but Larkin did not: Tennessee played LSU in Baton Rouge on Saturday. He phoned Lou Higgins and told him where the play-off would be. Higgins said, "That's great, because I need to see you," and promised to attend.

The team bus left for the coast at five on Friday morning. Larkin had told Emily he'd eat breakfast at Weber's Truckstop, but when the alarm woke him at 3:45, he smelled bacon and heard eggs sizzling. He put on his bathrobe and went downstairs.

Emily said, "Good morning."

"You didn't have to get up to cook my breakfast."

"I couldn't cook it lying down."

"You know what I mean."

She pressed the eggs with her spatula. "I thought coaches were naturally superstitious."

The morning of the opening game, Larkin had forgotten to brush his teeth. Every Friday since, he'd walked around with a dirty mouth. He said, "I guess some coaches are."

"Well, I've cooked your breakfast every Friday morning, and since the team's been winning, I think I better do it now. I don't want to stand between you and success."

They ate breakfast, drank coffee. He showered and packed his bag. On the way out, he kissed her and said, "See you Saturday evening."

"Sure," she said. "And good luck."

Indianola led 3–0 with two minutes left. Then Bay St. Louis switched to the shotgun, a formation they hadn't shown all year. Four times the quarterback hit his wide receivers in the seams between the zones. Ten seconds remained when the split end, running a pick, screened James Hill, who should've had the tailback man to man. The tailback caught the ball on the five and outran Larkin's safety.

"Tough luck," Higgins told him in the dressing room.

"It wasn't luck. They just beat us."

Higgins said, "Let's step outside."

In the parking lot, he said that Bill Battle planned to hire someone else to coach the defensive ends but he wanted Larkin to join the staff as strength coach. "Our weight room's not in great shape," he said, "but you'll be able to buy whatever equipment you want and design a program that suits you. You'll have a free hand."

Larkin said, "Ever see a grown man dance by himself?"

Since Battle would like to meet him, Higgins said, why not

catch a bus up to Baton Rouge for the game? He said the athletic department would pick up the tab for flying him home, so Larkin returned to the dressing room and asked Mason if he'd pick him up Sunday at the Greenville airport.

Mason said, "Sure. Anything up?"

"Coach Higgins invited me to see the Vols play." He preferred not to mention the job until he'd signed a contract. Anyhow, this was not the time; Mason had just coached his last game and lost. "Maybe if I watch enough good defense," he said, "I'll learn how to hang on when I'm ahead."

The team bused to the Gulfport Holiday Inn, which faced the beach. Mason stood at the front of the bus and announced that he planned to dip his feet in the water. Most of the players followed him.

Larkin said, "I'll be there in a minute." He entered the hotel and rode the elevator up to his room, where he called Delta Airlines and booked a flight. He was walking out when the phone rang.

Emily said, "It's me."

He'd resolved not to think of her tonight. Sooner or later, he knew, he'd have to tell her about the job at Tennessee. He recalled how she looked alone on the couch, a drink in her hand, the TV murmuring nonsense.

He said. "Hi. This is a nice surprise."

"I listened to the game on WNLA. I'm sorry, Jackie. But the defense played well."

He sat down on the bed. The best thing to do, he decided, was to tell her about the job right now. That way, he wouldn't have to dread it, and he wouldn't have to feel like he'd deceived her.

"The night wasn't a total loss," he said. "I got offered a college coaching job."

"Where?" Her voice sounded remote.

"The University of Tennessee."

"That's . . . well, that's wondeful. They have a good team, don't they?"

"Pretty good. They're six and two right now, but they've got LSU tomorrow night." He told her he planned to attend the game in Baton Rouge and then fly to Greenville Sunday evening.

He thought she might ask if he needed a ride. Instead she said, "Congratulations, Jackie. It's late. I think I'll say good-night."

He said, "Good-night, Emily . . . See you Sunday?"

"Sure," she said. "I'm not going anywhere."

•   •   •

He woke wanting to call her, but Mason lounged around the room drinking coffee and reading the sports until time to leave. The team bus unloaded Larkin at Trailways, so that he could board a bus to Baton Rouge.

Higgins met him in the lobby at the Hilton, then showed him up to Battle's room and introduced him. Battle chatted with him half an hour, his eyes darting from Larkin's face to the TV, where Alabama disassembled Kentucky. He said the coaching position would have to be advertised, but it was Larkin's if he wanted it. Larkin assured him he would kill for it.

At Tiger Stadium that evening, he walked the ramp to the mezzanine, begged change from a vendor, found a phone booth, and dialed Emily. No answer. She'd probably hauled the kids to a movie.

Tennessee won the game 17–10. Larkin stood atop the UT bench trying to keep track of the action, but he registered little save color and sound. Storms of Dixie beer cups bombarded the UT cheerleaders. A guy dressed up in a Tiger suit strutted the opposite sideline. The Tennessee band played "The Tennessee Waltz." And through it all Larkin thought of Emily. Clearly she cared about him. The question was, had she begun to count on him? No one had before, at least not for long, and he thought

Emily knew more about men than any other woman he'd known. She should have been able to size him up.

Mason dropped him off on Sunday evening at nine. Only the hall lamp lit the house. Emily had tacked a note to the door.

Jackie, the children are at Burt's. Unfortunately, I'm in bed with some sort of awful bug. I don't think you should come near me this evening. It might be contagious.

That night he slept badly. For one thing, he doubted that she was sick. She just wanted to avoid him. She had a history of recovering from injury, and this was probably the way she went about it, hiding till the hurt subsided.

Equally troubling to Larkin was his disappointment when he discovered he wouldn't see her this evening.

•   •   •

"Here you are." She handed him his plate. It contained a huge omelet.

Her eyes were clear, her hair neatly brushed. She leaned over, poured coffee into his cup. Then she sat and buttered her toast.

He said, "Feeling any better?"

"Yes."

"Think it was a virus?"

"Probably. Those things wipe me out for a day or so."

He sliced the omelet. "This must be an inch thick. Nobody else makes them like you do."

"Thanks."

"I might not go to Knoxville after all," he said.

"Oh?" She reached for the saltshaker. "Why's that?"

"I found out the school board's going to offer me Bill's job."

"That's nice." She salted the omelet, cut a wedge out, and ate it. "I'm surprised," she said, "that you'd rather have Bill's job than the one at Tennessee."

He said he found college coaches unsavory: they all wore

polyester suits, styled their hair like Glen Campbell, and paid their players on a per-tackle basis. Then he gazed at his omelet and added, "Plus, I don't really want to move away from here."

When she laid down her fork, it clicked against her plate. She said, "You love Indianola that much?"

"Not Indianola. *Here.*"

"Oh. You mean the house. You want to buy it?"

"You know what I mean."

"No. I don't."

He was sweating. Little rivers streamed from his armpits. He said, "I mean you."

"You want to buy me?"

"I want to live with you."

"You already live with me."

"I want to keep living with you."

"What if I raise the rent?"

"I can pay."

"Can you?"

Her lips hinted at a smile. He knew then that he loved her. The knowledge only terrified him a little bit. "Yes," he said, "I can." He licked his dry lips. "Maybe we ought to have a contract."

When she spoke, her voice was quiet. "I'd love to leave here with you," she said. "Really I would."

"So let's go," he said. "We'll toss the kids into suitcases and head north."

She said she couldn't: she had already told him why.

"I know," he said. Feeling jumpy, he swigged coffee, as if it might calm him.

"I hate to think of you leaving," she told him. She said he could probably imagine what life was like for a divorced woman with children, especially in a town this size. After a while you found yourself shopping Wal-Mart for excitement, and you began to hate Christmas. "But if you stay," she said, "I want it to be because you want to. I don't want you to hate me down the road."

Larkin knew he shouldn't hesitate. "I want to stay," he said. Fifty-one percent of him meant it. He would have to be content with majority rule.

•   •   •

They sat on the couch drinking coffee until almost eight o'clock. Before he left, they agreed to meet for lunch.

On the way to work he walked by Legion Field. The rickety bleachers seated two thousand. The dressing rooms—portable buildings purchased from Indianola Lumber Company—leaked and would soon need replacing. The field was hard and pocked. Every dry day during the summer, he and Mason hooked up sprinklers. Mason had done that for more than fifteen years.

Until now, Larkin had thought career high-school coaches lacked some essential ingredient; it was this deficiency that made them what they were. But when he stood near the wrought-iron fence and stared at the stadium, he formed a new opinion. It took something extra to do a good job year after year in a place like this. You had to believe in the divinity of effort.

When he walked into Emily's yard that afternoon, Richard was trying to place-kick. He charged the ball and squibbed it ten or twelve feet.

Larkin said, "You've got to get under it."

"Show me."

Picking up the ball, Larkin said, "Remember that time you told me I'd never coach the Dallas Cowboys?"

"Yeah. What about it?"

"You were right," Larkin said.

He teed up the ball and stepped backwards.

THE TRIP

FOR weeks I'd been excited about the trip to the Smokies. I'd never left the Delta and could scarcely imagine mountains. Pestering Dad, I drew steep inverted Vs, upended cones no creature could possibly climb, and asked, "Do they look like this?"

"They're not quite that steep."

Once I forced the pen on him. "Show me."

The slope he drew looked too gradual. "That ain't nothing," I said.

His square jaw locked, my pen shot toward the top of the page, then continued on, streaking over the tabletop. "How about that?" Dad demanded when he'd piloted the pen clean off the table. "You want to climb one bigger than that?"

"No sir!" I said. "Are we gonna see one like that?"

"We might," he said.

"Are we gonna go up it?"

"We might," he said again, "if anybody gets out of line. Anybody misbehaves at all, we'll find one just like that and head straight for the top."

We got up at three o'clock in the morning and ate breakfast. Then the three of us piled into the car, crowded with suitcases

and a Coleman stove and a Clorox box full of food. We headed for
Grandpa's house.

On the way Dad flipped on the CB that he'd installed especially for the trip. We heard Grandpa say, "You got a bed in your
truck?"

A woman's voice said, "Ten-four, honey. You got one in
yours?"

Grandpa sounded sad. "No, I don't have nothing but hoes in
mine. Reckon you'll be through here again? I sure would love to
see inside that camper."

Dad hit the switch. "Hey!" I hollered. "Who's he talking to?"

"Hush up," he said.

A minute or two later we wheeled into the yard. Grandpa's
blue Tempest stood parked beside the chinaberry tree. He was
sitting in the car, talking into the microphone, but the second he
saw us he put the mike down.

"Don't be nasty to him," Mother said. "Please."

Dad looked at her and said, "You really think I'm a monster,
don't you?"

Mother didn't say she did, and she didn't say she didn't. She
just stared down at her lap and said, "Just please don't be nasty
to him."

"Go in the house," Dad told her, "and make some coffee."

"You just had coffee."

"I want some more," he said.

She went inside the house. I followed Dad over to Grandpa's car.

Grandpa was tall like Dad but fat. One quarter Choctaw, he
had a red face, thick black eyebrows, and a beard so heavy he
always looked as if he hadn't shaved for three days. Though most
of the men in the community favored crew cuts back then, he
maintained a head of wavy hair barely tinged by grey. Once I
heard the barber ask him why he didn't get a crew cut, and he

said it was because he wanted to leave something for fingers to run through.

He said, "Hey, Pal-o-mine," and tossed me a Hershey bar.

"Luther," Dad said, "that radio ain't a toy. There's a penalty for what you just did."

"Aw, Mutt—just always trying to catch somebody."

"It so happens the license is in my name. If some FCC inspector heard you just now, I'll be the one that gets a pink slip in the mail."

"I didn't use no call letters."

Dad shook his head. "That's another violation," he said.

A few minutes later, when Mother returned, I jumped into the Tempest with Grandpa. Dad saw what I was up to. I halfway hoped he'd order me in with him and Mother, just so I could pitch a big fit.

Instead he showed me his back. It was broad.

•   •   •

That first day on the road I saw another state for the first time. Just after sunrise we crossed the Alabama line. The road rolled over hills beneath a canopy of pine. We passed through towns called Guin, Jasper, Cullman.

I asked Grandpa if he'd been to Alabama before, and he said, "Yeah. Your grandma had folks over close to Birmingham. You remember your Aunt Hazel?"

I didn't. I didn't even remember Grandma too well, though I knew from pictures that she was almost as tall as Grandpa, that she had bright red hair, and that she almost always wore big earbobs.

Thinking about Grandma made me remember my favorite story. "Tell about the time," I said, "when Grandma tried to shoot Ed Sullivan."

"That was the year you come into this world," he said. "1962.

See, James Meredith, a colored fellow, wanted to go to college at Ole Miss. And Ross Barnett—he was the governor—he tried to stop him.

"Well, that made John Kennedy mighty mad. So he went on TV on Sunday night and told everybody he didn't mean maybe, he wanted Meredith enrolled. Said he'd call out the National Guard if he had to.

"After Kennedy went off, your grandma she got to talking on the phone with Mae Snow, and Mae said she'd heard folks was taking guns and going to Oxford to keep Meredith out. So your grandma comes in the living room where I'm watching Ed Sullivan and tries to hand me the shotgun. Claims I ought to go to Oxford and fight for States' Rights. I just laid the gun on the floor and laughed at her.

"She says, 'What are you, a man or a mouse?' I told her I'd let her know once Ed went off the air.

"Well, she hoisted that old shotgun to her shoulder and aimed it straight at Ed. Said, 'Either you get up and go to Oxford, or I'll blow that ugly Ed Sullivan to Hell.'"

"And then," I said, picking up the narrative, "you took the gun and got in the pickup and drove over to Mr. Hill's house."

"And watched the rest of Ed Sullivan," said Grandpa, "and then I took a good long nap. Next morning I went home and told her I'd done my part."

"And what'd she say?"

"She didn't say anything. She just did her best to show me how happy I'd made her."

"How?"

He grinned at the windshield. "Just by doing two or three little deeds for me."

I imagined her rubbing his back or fluffing his pillow for him, like Mother did for me. I was glad he'd had someone to do that.

"I like that story a lot," I said. "It's true, ain't it?"

"Partly," he said. "Why don't you take a little nap?"

So I took a little nap, and when I woke we were facing the mountains.

•   •   •

They were impressive from a distance—high and green, with rock ledges here and there—but the closer you got, the smaller they seemed. But then, when you were actually on top of them and you saw the tiny houses below and eighteen-wheelers looking like toy trucks on the road, they became impressive once more.

Atop Lookout Mountain, south of Chattanooga, we stopped at a roadside park to eat lunch. While Mother made sandwiches and Dad poked around under the car hood, I grabbed my football and tossed it to Grandpa. He promptly tossed it back.

"Run a down-and-out," I ordered.

He didn't actually run, just shuffled along, his big work shoes never clearing the ground. He took about a minute to cover five yards. Near an overflowing trash can, he veered left.

I had a strong arm for a seven-year-old. I hit him right in the gut. For once, he held on to the ball.

"I'm going long!" I yelled, but as I turned to run, Dad called, "Come here."

I made the mistake of stomping the ground.

His faced bloomed rosy. He opened his mouth to growl, "Make haste!" but he never had to do it, because when I saw the color of his cheeks, haste was exactly what I made.

He was holding a white rag. He carried such rags wherever he went, along with a can of Go-jo for cleaning his hands.

He calmed down pretty quickly this time. "We need to check our oil," he said. "Look there: see our little stick?"

To him, everything was ours and everything was little: our little oilcan, our little stick. It made me sick. I wanted everything to be mine, and I wanted it to be big.

"We pull the little stick out like this," he said, pulling it out.

"Then look—see where it says *safe?* If there's oil, like there is now, it means our engine ain't thirsty. But if the oil was down to where it says *add one,* we'd have to add one quart of oil. We've got some little cans in the trunk."

He was always trying to teach me the most uninteresting things—how to change the oil, how to mow the lawn. He never told stories like Grandpa.

I waited until he'd replaced our little stick. Then I said, "Are you through? I want to play football."

He wiped his hands on the rag. "Yeah," he said. "I guess I'm done with you. For now, anyhow."

Grandpa was sitting at the picnic table with Mother. The football lay in his lap.

I yelled, "I'm going long!" and took off.

•   •   •

We made North Carolina about six that evening. The mountains here dwarfed those in Tennessee and Alabama. Blue and hazy, they climbed into the clouds.

"They look like boar hogs, don't they?" said Grandpa. "Good golly, look way off over yonder," and he trained his finger on a distant monster.

We were driving east on Highway 19, which follows the Nantahala River through western North Carolina. To our left, the ground fell away, swooping toward white water far below. As I stared with Grandpa at the highest of the mountains, I suddenly felt the Tempest drifting into the left lane. "Grandpa!" I wailed.

He wrenched the steering wheel, jerking us into the right lane and throwing me against the door.

"Lordy," he whispered. "Did I hurt you?"

"No sir."

"I like to forgot where I was going. Too much pretty scenery."

Dad's voice sizzled over the CB. "What in hell's going on back there?"

Grandpa reached for the mike, but I snatched it away. Keying it, I said, "A squirrel ran in front of us."

"I didn't see no squirrel," he said.

The lie I'd told thrilled me. It was easy to be brave when the highway lay between us. "Well, there was a squirrel," I said. "Had the bushiest tail I ever seen."

He said nothing more. I glanced up at Grandpa, proud of myself, but he was frowning. "You ought not fib to your daddy," he said.

If he'd drawn his belt and thrashed me, he couldn't have hurt me worse. I'd lied to protect him.

I sank into the car seat to sulk.

•   •   •

We stopped for the night at Jenny's Motel.

Halfway between Bryson City and Cherokee and right across the highway from a grand-looking place called the Marked Tree Lodge, Jenny's was little more than two dingy buildings that faced each other across a slag-covered parking lot. Each of the buildings had seven or eight rooms. The office was number 1, the first room in the building closest the highway.

Sitting in the car with Grandpa, I watched Dad sign the register and pay for our room. The lady at the desk was tall and big bosomed. She had coal-black hair like Grandpa's. Red earrings dangled from her lobes.

"That woman looks like an Indian," I said to Grandpa, who I'd forgiven for turning against me.

He studied her. "Yeah," he said. "And I bet she keeps a mighty warm tepee."

Our room was number 14. It contained two beds, an armchair, an old gas range, and a refrigerator. In a nook between the kitchen area and the bathroom stood a rickety table with three black plastic chairs.

Mother asked, "What does everybody want to eat?"

"Hamburgers," I said.

"Hamburgers," Grandpa said.

She didn't wait to ask Dad. He was outside, unloading the car, and anyway he never cared what he ate. The previous year, when Mother had pneumonia, he'd fed me boiled weenies each night for a week.

Mother cooked the hamburgers and fried some onions. The air filled up with good smells. In the bathroom Grandpa showered and sang "The Wabash Cannonball." The only bad thing in all the world was that the room had no TV, the motel no pool.

"I wish this place had a TV," I said. "And a pool like the place across the road."

Dad lay on one of the beds, staring at the ceiling. "Just be glad you've got a roof over your head," he said. "I ain't Republican, buddy."

After supper, Mother told me to go brush my teeth. When I came back from doing it, Grandpa was gone. Dad was still lying on the bed, and Mother was sitting beside him, scratching his head, which was one thing both of us hated to do. He had a prickly flattop that he greased twice a day with Vitalis; at the end of a two-hour session, your hand would feel as if you'd dipped it in Crisco.

When she saw me, Mother rolled her eyes toward the ceiling. This meant, roughly, *I'm really unlucky.* We had a whole system of signs. If she puckered her lips and halfway closed her left eye at the supper table, it meant I should shut up because Dad didn't like what I was saying.

I knew that if I didn't escape right now, he'd soon draft me for the head-scratching brigade. I asked, "Can I go out and kick the football a while?"

"Yeah," he said, "if you'll promise me you'll stay away from the road."

Outside it was almost dark. I looked around for Grandpa. There were some metal lawn chairs at one end of our building, and I thought he might be there, but I found them empty. So I walked across the parking lot.

There were lawn chairs at one end of the other building too, and Grandpa was sitting in one of them, next to the woman from the office. I squatted behind some bushes to listen.

"You better believe it," the woman was saying. "I sure *have* seen some stuff. I opened this place almost twenty years ago, and in that time I bet I've lost ten thousand towels. Theft, pure and simple. Anything in a motel room that's not bolted down, I guarantee you somebody'll steal it. They'll take the sheets, take the lamps, rip the rugs off the floor. One time my cleaning girl come told me, 'Miss Jenny, somebody done pilfered the commode from number 6.' Damn if they hadn't. Whoever took it must have been a plumber. He'd shut everything off real nice. I'm just waiting for somebody to steal a bed."

"I'd hold on to them beds," said Grandpa. "Them beds can be put to good use."

Miss Jenny looked at Grandpa. Grandpa grinned. It was a funny kind of grin.

Miss Jenny said, "You trying to tell me you're a ladies' man?"

"There's them that says I am and them that says I ain't."

"And I bet you don't waste time on them that say you ain't."

"I'd fix a flat for 'em," said Grandpa, "if they was to have a blowout a long ways from town."

Miss Jenny made a fist and chucked Grandpa's shoulder. "I don't know what's come over me the last two or three years," she said. "Been a Christian lady all my life, but lately I got so I just love such as this."

Grandpa stared at her chest. Even I knew you weren't supposed to do that.

"Bet you get plenty of chances, don't you?" he said.

Miss Jenny smiled and said, "A few."

"What do you do when you get a chance?"

"Sometimes," she said, "I up and take it."

Grandpa stared at Heaven, sighed, and said, "I wish this was one of them times."

"You want a little toddy?" she asked him.

They stood up together. Grandpa put his arm around her shoulders, and the two of them disappeared around the corner of the building.

I eased over to the corner and peeped around it. The door to room 2 was just closing.

•   •   •

A couple of days later, while driving through Asheville, North Carolina, Grandpa and I got lost in heavy traffic.

"What if they don't know we're not behind them?" I said. "They might drive on a long way."

"I imagine they've missed us," Grandpa said. "But we're low on gas anyhow. We'll stop at a service station and call 'em on the CB."

He pulled off at a Gulf station and picked up the mike. "Mutt?" he said. "This is Luther. Can y'all hear me?"

There was silence for a time. Then Dad said, "KBR 7945. Unit one to unit two."

"Here I am," Grandpa said. "Where y'all at?"

"Unit two," Dad said, "you need to follow correct on-air procedure. Please comply."

"Ah Lordy," Grandpa whispered. He keyed the mike and said, "KBR 7945. Unit two to unit one."

"This is unit one," Dad said. "Over."

"Unit one," Grandpa said, "where are you?"

Dad said, "I'm at the Texaco station across the street."

When Grandpa looked across the street and saw Dad, it made

him so mad he slammed the mike down. "What in the world," he raged, "what in the world makes that man behave that way?"

I began pondering Grandpa's question, and by the end of that day, I'd arrived at an answer. Dad was the way he was because Mother and I didn't want to scratch his head, and he knew it. And Grandpa was the way he was because even a stranger like Miss Jenny would invite him into her room and rub his back and fluff his pillow.

That very night, at a motel in Hillsville, Virginia, I made Dad's pillow plump as a butterball turkey. And when he emerged from the shower, I was standing by his bed. On my right hand I wore a Glad sandwich bag.

"What are you up to?" he said.

"I'm gonna scratch your head."

"Not with that bag you're not. What did you do to my pillow?"

He mashed it flat and lay down.

With dwindling hope, I asked, "Do you want me to rub your back?"

"No," he said. "I want you to hush and let me get some sleep."

So he slept and Mother slept and Grandpa slept too. Only I lay awake.

After a while I nudged Grandpa. He muttered, "Huh?"

"What did you and that woman do the other night?" I asked. "In room number 2 at the motel."

He clamped his palm over my mouth.

Before I could start struggling, he put his lips to my ear and whispered, "If I tell you, will you promise not to tell nobody?"

I nodded.

He took his hand off my mouth. "It was exercises," he whispered.

"What kind of exercises?"

"Side-straddle hops, push-ups, hip thrusts—you name it."

"That's all?"

"That's all," he said.

In the morning, when Dad woke, I said, "You want to do some side-straddle hops?"

He said, "Hell no."

It was then that I knew it was hopeless.

A GREEN CARD

MARYLA is on her best behavior. When Tom picked her up this afternoon, he said, "This party tonight is strictly civilian. No military personnel allowed." He meant that she should issue no commands. He told her that he had been mad at her for a week or two and that lately, whenever he walked into the kitchen and heard Nina speaking Polish on the phone, he would snap to attention and if she was talking to Maryla, Nina would smile and nod. "I'm not telling you this to hurt you," he said. "I'm telling you this because I think you're doing yourself in."

"I can't help it," she said. "That's the way I am."

"I'm going to help you help it. First of all, I'm not changing your light bulb again unless you say please. And I don't want you to ask me again—although you never really asked; you ordered— I don't want you to ask me to bring the damn Memphis paper up to the school. If I bring it, I bring it. If I don't, I don't. And please, Maryla, when Harry starts telling you how he feels about Poland, don't tell him how you feel about it."

"I don't feel any way about it," she said.

"I know," Tom said, "and that's what I don't want you to tell him."

Now she's at Tom and Nina's, sitting on the couch beside

Harry, who is telling her how he feels about Poland. He's a tall man—gangly, one might say—and his hollow cheeks make him look malnourished. Periodically, he has told her, he fasts. According to the newspaper *Tygodnik Powszechny*, four "noncriminal" prisoners have been on a hunger strike in Mokotowskie Prison. For twenty-four hours each week Harry doesn't eat. He says it's his way of showing he supports them. "I'd like to do more," he says. "I've been writing letters to newspaper editors all over the country, but none of them ever get published."

Since 1982, when he was sent back to America for consorting with Solidarity activists, Harry has been a professor of biology at a small college in Virginia. Routinely, according to Tom, he lectures his students on political oppression and chastizes them for being apathetic. The only thing that keeps the college from firing him is that he's a whiz in his field, the author of three textbooks and more than a hundred articles.

"You should be careful," Maryla says. "You'll find yourself in a hospital or maybe even worse, and then you won't be able to return to Poland."

His chin droops toward the funny little string tie he's wearing. "They'll never let me come back," he says. "There's no use kidding myself."

Afraid he's going to weep, Maryla looks away. The house is full of Poles tonight. Most of them are here at the University of Mississippi on an exchange program. Harry was stopping over on his way back to Virginia from a conference in New Orleans, so Tom arranged the party to give him a chance to be around Polish people again. Maryla knows the party was also arranged to bring her into contact with an eligible American male.

Catching Tom's eye, she starts to tell him to play *First Circle* by Pat Metheny, then remembers that he promised to salute her, before everybody, if she barked orders.

"Tom," she says, trying to make her eyelashes flutter like she's seen Nina's do, "would you play my favorite record?"

Later, when only she and Tom and Nina and Harry and a woman named Jola are left, Tom starts acting drunk. He gets up, stumbles, leans against the wall, and giggles. Then he disappears.

Harry has put his arm around her. "You know who you remind me of?" he says. "Meryl Streep."

She can't believe two men have said that to her in less than three months. The first was a graduate student named Robert, who kept hanging around her when she first came here; he offered her rides home, took her grocery shopping, invited her to ball games and to The Gin, and then, mysteriously, quit having anything to do with her. Now, when she passes him in the hall, he usually looks the other way.

"Meryl Streep?" she says. "I can't believe that."

"I've enjoyed myself," Jola says. "But I have to be going."

When Jola stands, so does Maryla. "Where's Tom?" she asks Nina.

"I think he might have passed out."

Maryla doesn't believe Tom is drunk. "He has to take me home," she says.

"I'll drive you," Harry offers.

"Jola is going," Maryla says, suddenly feeling scared. "She'll drop me."

She pretends not to see Nina frowning at her.

Harry helps her into her sheepskin. "Okay if I give you a call?" he asks her.

"Of course."

"I wish I could stay another day," he says. "This damn job of mine."

Maryla thinks someone as kooky as he is ought to be grateful for having a job. But she doesn't say so. She just smiles at him and lets him kiss her cheek.

•   •   •

A year ago, her mother died. She had been sick for almost four years, and for most of that time Maryla had slept on a cot near her bed and taken care of her.

Her father was a foreman at the refrigerator factory. He had belonged to the Party since 1948, and he made good money. He could afford vodka even when half a liter cost five hundred zloty. During the strikes of '80 and '81, workers jeered him at the plant gates. When he came home in the evenings, he would sit down in the living room and drink for hours, muttering about "deportations" and "the way things were in the fifties."

The windows in the living room arched almost to the ceiling. He was usually too drunk to climb the ladder and clean them. Maryla plied him with coffee. Finally he wobbled up the ladder while she tried to steady it. Once, perched eight rungs up, he gazed down at her and for the only time in her adult life he offered her advice.

"Stay away from those fools."

"Which fools?" she said. "There are so many."

"You know who I mean."

She did. Everybody in her department except her had joined Solidarity.

"Don't you worry about that," she told him. "I'm not interested in politics. I'm interested in your cleaning those windows."

The apartment was a large one. But back in the sixties, when Maryla was nine or ten, the municipal authorities had decreed that another lodger must move in. The new tenant was a small redheaded woman. Jagoda was her name, and she worked in an office at the Copernicus Museum. At home, she used her own entrance; she ate her meals and took her baths an hour earlier than the family. Somehow, in the early seventies, she acquired a telephone. She told Maryla's mother they were welcome to use it. Each morning, when she left for work, she removed the phone from her room and placed it on a table in the hall.

When Maryla's mother got sick, Jagoda sometimes shopped for Maryla. She pulled warm loaves of bread from her plastic shopping bag, took out fruits and vegetables she'd purchased at the market. She did it without being asked, and at first Maryla was grateful for the favors. But after a while she began to regard them as her due. Hearing Jagoda's door close, she would put out her head and holler, "Wait! I need bay leaf!"

She did everything possible to avoid the queues. Her aunt worked at a meat market; it was illegal, but she agreed to take Maryla's coupons, cut meat for her—almost all of it first-quality—and pass it to her out the back of the store. On the sidewalk in front of the store, old veterans halted her. They didn't have to queue, they could take your coupons and for a price retrieve your meat immediately. When they offered, Maryla shook her head and pushed past them, thinking, *I'm a veteran too.*

She had been to the meat market the day she came home and found the old lady who sometimes watched her mother wringing her hands. "I can't tell if she's breathing," she said.

Maryla went into the bedroom. Her mother was certainly breathing, but her pulse seemed weak.

"Where's Father?" she said.

"He hasn't come."

She wanted to call the doctor, but Jagoda had withdrawn the phone. She pounded on the door. When Jagoda opened it, Maryla saw her father sitting in a chair by the window, the motion of his teacup arrested.

"Call Dr. Bronkowska," Maryla ordered. She turned her back on the scene, but the image lingered, and a few days later she saw her father walking with Jagoda along the Vistula.

She never saw him enter her room again, but she did see them talking in the courtyard, and once, near the Market Square, she thought she saw them board a tram.

She suspected that when her mother died, her father and Jagoda would marry. She couldn't imagine a future for herself.

Back before her mother got sick, she had dated a man for almost two years. Wacek had told her many times how much he loved her. She decided she loved him too, and she made up her mind to marry him when he asked.

He never asked. He went on vacation to West Berlin and wrote after three weeks to say he wouldn't be back. *It isn't you I want to leave,* he wrote. *It's Poland.*

"If it was only Poland he wanted to leave," said her mother, "he could ask you to come to him. You wouldn't bring Poland with you." She said that she had never liked Wacek; he seemed unreliable. She said he reminded her of her Uncle Zygmunt, who was a dentist in Lithuania and a drunkard who once almost killed a patient by giving him gas and then going into his office and getting drunk and forgetting about him.

Now everyone Maryla knew was married. They attended parties as couples. When she received an invitation to a party, she either had to refuse or, if she went, leave early. Her acquaintances discussed the theater, the underground press, and above all, politics, things for which she had no time. Before the '84 elections, people were vocal about their intentions not to vote. One night at a party, as if to spite them all, she announced, "*I'm* going to vote."

The room grew quiet. Someone said, "How can you?"

She was afraid not to. If she didn't, they might put her name on a list somewhere and it might cost her a chance at an apartment. When her mother died, getting an apartment of her own would be the most important thing.

"I have worries enough," she said.

A Jewish psychologist was present. He had been interned in 1981 for serving as adviser to striking workers at the Warek carriage works. "A lot of people who were interned had old sick parents," he said. "Me, for instance."

She wished she had kept her mouth shut. Everyone was watching her. She attempted a joke.

"Yes," she said, "and what an embarrassment you must have been to them. A jailbird son."

Nobody laughed. Someone said, "Maryla is curiously free from ideological constraint."

Then everybody laughed. The laughter didn't sound particularly good-natured.

After that night, her invitations were fewer. When her mother died, she gave up the idea of buying an apartment. She didn't have enough money, and she hated Poland anyway.

She had two friends in the U.S. One of them, Kasia, owned and ran a janitorial service in San Francisco, and she had written Maryla that she could come and work for her. The other friend, Nina, had gone to Mississippi on an academic exchange program, and when she got there she had met and married an American.

Maryla wrote to Nina. She didn't want to scrub anyone else's bathroom, not even a bathroom overlooking the Bay. What she wanted was an easier and more pleasant life.

Two weeks before she left, her father said he would marry Jagoda.

•   •   •

The morning after the party at which she met Harry, Maryla is awakened by a knock on her door.

It's a delivery boy with a dozen red roses. The note says, *You're nice.* The roses are from Harry.

She takes out one of the crystal vases she brought from Poland. She fills the vase with water, puts the long-stem roses in it, stands the vase on a table in the living room.

It's ten-thirty here, eight-thirty on the West Coast, but Kasia is an early riser. Maryla decides to give her a call.

"It's me," she says when Kasia answers.

"You sound funny."

"I just woke up."

"You're getting lazy here," Kasia says. "This country is robbing you of all your good qualities."

Nina has said the same thing about Kasia. In Poland, Kasia ran a small art gallery, read every book she could find on German Expressionism, maintained the largest collection of bebop records in Torun, and saw at least three films a week. Now she rents a townhouse for eighteen hundred dollars a month. She votes Republican, pays her employees minimum wage, and already is making plans to retire to Palm Springs. She came to America with a backpack.

"I met a man last night," Maryla tells her, "and he's interested in me."

"Did you sleep with him?"

"I said I met him last night."

"Maryla," says Kasia, "between last night and now lie these little things called hours."

"You know me better than that."

"Is this guy an American?"

Maryla says yes.

"Well," says Kasia, "the thing you have to learn about Americans is that they don't waste time. You meet a guy, you go to bed with him that night, and two or three weeks later, if everything is still moving okay, you get around to introducing yourselves. What's the guy like?"

Maryla, in describing him, leaves out the part about how he starves himself. As she talks about him, she realizes that there isn't a thing about him that appeals to her. He's a nut, he's too tall, he dresses funny, and he's forty, eight years older than she is. She tries to make him sound a little better than he is.

Kasia isn't impressed. "A professor," she says. "That's great, Maryla, if you want to live somewhere in a nice little two-bedroom house and pile into the station wagon with him and the kids once a year and go spend a week at the beach. You'll stay at a Holiday Inn and dine nightly at Bonanza. You ought to come out here like

I've been telling you. I'll buy you a ticket out, I'll train you, and when you've learned the business, you'll be my manager."

"You know I don't have a green card."

"I'll find an American to marry you for the green card. You know perfectly well that's how I got mine. California's full of bleeding hearts who want to *help* people. You'd get married, stay married just long enough to get the card, then get the divorce. You wouldn't even have to pay the guy. I can think of at least three candidates right now."

Maryla says she'll think about it. She changes the subject and a few minutes later says good-bye. Clearly, Kasia thinks nobody worth a broken coin would marry her out of any impulse but charity.

For the rest of the day she feels like a refugee.

•   •   •

The next day, Sunday, she and Nina attend mass.

Because she divorced her Polish husband and married Tom, Nina doesn't take communion, and she's told Maryla that being unable to participate in the ritual is bothering her. Maryla thinks that's silly. She knows Nina isn't particularly religious, so she can't understand this attachment to Catholic ritual and tradition. To her, the only traditions that matter are the little ones you devise for yourself. She always vacuums the apartment on Saturdays. She eats pork for dinner at least three times a week, she goes to the Twin Cinema on Monday (bargain night), she handles correspondence, when there is any, on Thursday, and she shops for groceries on Friday, and always at Kroger. When she first came to America, her life was a shapeless mess; but within weeks, through repetition, she had achieved definition.

After church, she walks home with Nina. They go by way of the Square. It's February, but it's so warm that a couple of old men are sitting on a bench in front of the courthouse, and they aren't even wearing their jackets.

"Look at that," Nina says. "The middle of winter, and it's warm enough to go sunbathing. Last night I called my mother. She said it was minus twelve in Torun, and there's been snow every day for two weeks. I miss Poland."

"I'm glad it's warm here," Maryla says. "It keeps down heating bills."

Nina sighs, "Oh, Maryla," and shakes her head.

Maryla thinks that if Nina had to live on a graduate assistant's salary, she might enjoy warmth too. She spent all her savings coming here. Now she has 232 dollars in the bank, and she's living from hand to mouth. Her visa is good until July, at which point she can get an extension for one more year; then, assuming her circumstances haven't changed, she'll have to return to Poland. If she goes back without the money to buy an apartment, her life won't be worth living. Right now, she's about five thousand American dollars short.

Nina fixes lunch for her and Tom. Tom sits at the kitchen table, across from Maryla, and follows Nina with his eyes. "When I met Nina," he says now, "she was skin and bones."

"Baloney," says Nina, who has learned American slang.

"Really," he tells Maryla. "The first time I went to bed with her, her hip bones hurt me. They were just jutting out. But I fattened her up, and now she's prime."

"He fed me Crisco burgers," says Nina. "That was all he could cook."

"It looks like you've made a conquest," Tom tells Maryla. "Harry was singing your praises yesterday morning."

Maryla wishes Harry were more like Tom. Though at first it shocked her, she's come to like the way Tom strings together four or five curse words at a time, in a train of jovial obscenity. When Maryla first came here, he made all her arrangements. He rented her apartment, opened her bank account, registered her for classes, and took her to Kroger. She likes the way he looks, too.

"Harry's *okay*," she says now. "But I'm not interested in him."
Nina turns away from the counter. "Why not?"

She said it as if it were ridiculous for Maryla not to be interested. Maryla knows Nina and Harry were friends in Poland, but she doesn't think that's the reason for Nina's reaction. Nina just believes she ought to be interested in anybody who's interested in her. Nina thinks she can't be choosy.

"Oh, he's all right," she says. "But not for me."

Nina turns her back. Her ponytail flounces; her apron strings swish.

•   •   •

In the next three weeks, Harry phones her nine times. He always begins by asking if he woke her, even though he never calls later than nine, and he always speaks to her in Polish.

She discovers that he's been married and divorced twice, not once like she thought. Both wives were Poles. The first one left him in 1976 because she could no longer stand living in Poland and Harry refused to leave it; he wasn't going to give up his country for her. The second wife and he were doing just fine until he started distributing leaflets for Solidarity. When the SB arrested him, she testified against him.

"I remember that," Maryla says. "She was on TV. She said you were operating a powerful illegal broadcast center."

"I had an AM radio in my study," he says. "It didn't even work."

Switching to English, she uses one of Tom's expressions. "It sounds like Poland kicked your ass. Why do you love it so much?"

"The best ten years of my life were spent in Poland," he says. He tells her that he went there as a tourist, jut wanting to see the country where his grandfather was born, and he fell so much in love with the place that he applied for permanent residence. "There's so much raw life in Poland," he says, "and the people are so friendly. Whenever I took my coupons to the meat market, the butchers would always try to give me nothing but first-quality cuts because they could tell I was a foreigner. I always refused—I said, 'Hey, thanks, but I'm a Pole now too.' One time I was traveling through Nowy Targ on market day, and an old peasant lady tried to *give* me a sheep."

"If you had been a real Pole," says Maryla, "you would have taken that sheep and bartered it for coffee. Or dollars."

"Here in America people just shut themselves up in their houses," he says. "You can't get close to anybody—they're too busy watching 'Dallas.'"

"I watch 'Dallas,'" Maryla says, but he seems not to have heard her.

"What about you?" he says. "Surely you don't intend to stay here."

She's noncommittal. "Maybe. I don't know yet."

"You'd be losing so much if you stayed."

That remark makes her angry. She's on the verge of telling him that *she'd* be losing nothing. Then she thinks that having nothing to lose is embarrassing.

He says that since he can't make any friends here—"because everybody thinks I'm a kook"—what he probably needs is a family. He says that if he had a wife and kids, at least there would be someone at home to talk to.

But American women, he says, are so plastic.

●　　　●　　　●

"That sounds like a proposal," Kasia says from California. "A not very subtle one. How long were you around this guy?"

"Four or five hours."

"And you didn't even go to bed with him. Did you *talk* about bed?"

"Of course not."

"It sounds," says Kasia, "like he just wants a Polish woman. Any one will do."

Maryla feels reduced to a geographical accident.

"What you ought to do," says Kasia, "is send this guy a tape of *Sophie's Choice* and tell him to get lost."

A warning quiver at Maryla's mouth. "What's the weather like?" she says.

"It's raining. Maryla, why don't you let me send you a ticket? I'll teach you the business from the ground up—actually, from the bathroom tiles up, but then you never minded work—and in a couple of years you'll become my manager. You could buy a car—you could even buy a house. Then you won't have to depend on some guy who thinks he's Pilsudski."

Maryla tells her she'll think about it, and this time she means it. She wants to settle her future as soon as possible. The idea of owning a house, of having something permanent, something of her own, is appealing. Maybe she would hire herself a servant.

When she unlocks her mailbox, there's a letter from her father. *Jagoda,* he writes, *sends you wishes. She's moved a few things around in our part of the place. Of course, it's actually all ours now, and I'm glad. I hate any kind of partition.*

•   •   •

On the Monday prior to Easter, Harry calls. After asking if he woke her—it's 8 P.M.—he says he's been thinking of coming down for the holiday.

This afternoon, Maryla visited Nina, and Nina said, "When I met Tom he didn't interest me in the slightest. He thought it was reactionary to care about appearance. He always wore whatever clothes his grandmother bought him for Christmas, and she prefers polyester because it's man-made—Tom says her taste in clothes is humanistic.

"I could hardly understand him because of that awful Delta accent. I've never liked big men. I went to dinner with him hoping that if I tried my best to bore him he'd leave me alone. I started liking him while we were eating dessert. I ended up in bed with him that night and that's where I've been every night since then. You don't have anything to lose by just giving someone a chance."

It was clear which someone she meant; the someones hadn't exactly formed a queue.

Maryla thought this afternoon that maybe Nina was right. Now she thinks that Harry probably asked Nina to talk to her before he called to propose his visit. To her that seems adolescent. He probably isn't a man to be relied on.

She says, "That's a long way to drive for a weekend."

"I'd fly."

"Wouldn't that be expensive?"

"Not really."

"It costs seven hundred dollars to fly from here to California."

"I didn't know you'd been to California."

"I haven't."

"Well, I can fly to Memphis and back for under two hundred dollars. There are special rates this weekend."

She wonders if he expects special rates when he gets here. Does he think she's been marked down?

She knows she has. And the forces that devalued her aren't getting any weaker. Whenever she imagines returning to her father's apartment, where Jagoda presides, sleeping in her mother's bed, her stomach crawls into her throat.

"I'm not busy this weekend," she says.

"Would you mind if I came down?"

She tries to sound enthusiastic, ends up screaming, "Of course not!"

They talk for a few more minutes. Before he hangs up, he says he'll call Tom and ask him to pick him up in Memphis. Nothing is said about whose place he'll stay at.

•   •   •

Wednesday night, Tom phones and asks Maryla to ride to Memphis with him Saturday for the purpose of retrieving Harry.

She says, "I can't. That's when I clean the apartment."

"Clean it Friday night."

"That's when I shop."

"Shop on Thursday."

"Thursday I answer my letters."

"Jesus!" Tom says. "You're a metronome."

The real reason she doesn't want to go is that she's been feeling scared and embarrassed, and she wants to put off seeing Harry as long as she can. She knows Tom and Nina mean well, but she's become aware that they pity her. They're behaving as if they hope to sell her.

Harry and Tom arrive at lunchtime. They all four eat at Nina's. Harry mentions plans he has to start a magazine that will cover the freedom movement in Poland. He asks Tom what he thinks of the project.

"It's a worthwhile idea," Tom says, "but it isn't too easy to start a magazine."

"You know what would make a great cover for the first issue?" Harry says excitedly. "A likeness of Walesa—or Michnik, maybe, since he's always in jail—no, Walesa's more recognizable—you'd have a picture of him with a crown of barbed wire around his forehead. Blood would be trickling down his cheeks."

"I'd think about this carefully," Tom warns.

"What do you think?" Harry asks Maryla.

"I think you're crazy," she says without thinking. Then, "I mean—"

He isn't insulted. He laughs. "Everybody thinks that," he says. "If everybody thinks it, it's probably so."

While Nina takes Harry out to show him her garden, Maryla helps Tom clear the table.

"What do you see in him?" she asks.

"Harry? I see decency in him. Look, I know he's a little wacky right now, but it's going to take him a while to get over what happened in Poland. He was happy there."

Happy in Poland is a concept Maryla can't grasp. It makes as much sense as *hot in Siberia.*

She and Tom wash the dishes. Harry and Nina return soon, and Nina says it's time to go to church.

Because there are several Polish people in Oxford, the priest has agreed to conduct a special service for blessing the eggs. Nina is proud of her basket, which is small and delicate, shaped like a canoe. She says she and Tom spent two hours last night scratching designs on the eggs. Tom made his look like footballs, she drew flowers on hers. Harry surprises them with two red eggs he brought from Virginia. He's scratched squiggly lines all over them.

"I'm the Jackson Pollock," he says, "of Easter-egg art."

After church they return to Tom and Nina's. Harry excuses himself, goes out to Tom's car, comes back a moment later with a bottle of Wyborowa.

Nina claps her hands. "Real Polish vodka!"

"You can't buy it here," says Tom.

"I found it in Richmond," Harry says, opening the bottle.

Maryla is thinking that he probably brought the bottle in his suitcase, and since he went to the car to get it, that's probably where his bag still is.

They drink for an hour, talking about the people they all know in Poland. Harry wants to speak Polish, but Nina reminds him that Tom's Polish is at best rudimentary.

"Mostly," Tom says, "I know swear words."

"Do you have any Polish music?"

Tom plays Ewa Demarczyk. It's a scratchy live recording that Nina says was made at the Jewish Theater in Warsaw. When Demarczyk sings "Pocalunki," Harry asks Maryla to dance.

She says, "It isn't the kind of thing you dance to, and I don't dance."

"Sure you do," he says and pulls her off the couch.

He turns her slowly. Soon Tom and Nina are up, swaying beside them. That isn't so terrible. But then there's a brief pause, and the next thing she knows she's spinning wildly; the walls are turning, bookcases rush past her, *War and Peace* zips by; pounding gypsy rhythms rock the room, Demarczyk is trilling and shouting, Tom and Nina are clapping their hands.

Harry whirls her round and round; she knows how a stroke victim feels.

Later, she and Harry sit on the couch while Tom and Nina fix dinner. It's dusky outside. There's a strange odor in the air; she wonders if it's honeysuckle. Shyly, Harry asks if he can stay at her place this evening.

She says okay.

•   •   •

In the apartment above hers, a loud party is taking place. People up there are dancing.

"The light will probably go out," she says. "When they start stomping the floor, that's what happens. I can't reach the fixture, even if I stand on the couch, so when it happens I have to call Tom."

"Well, if it goes out," Harry says, "I'll change it."

They're sipping wine now. He puts his arm around her.

"You ought to come visit me in Virginia," he says. "I've got this great old farmhouse on a mountain above the New River. The New River is one of the oldest rivers in the world. When you go wading in it, you can feel the age of the rocks beneath your feet."

He leans over to kiss her, very tentative. She knew he would be that way. When their lips meet, the light quivers a couple of times and goes out.

"I wonder what that means?" says Harry.

She stands, feels her way into the kitchen. Then she flips on the light and takes a fresh bulb from the cabinet. She walks back into the living room and hands Harry the new bulb. He stands on a chair and begins unscrewing the globe. Maryla watches him a second, says, "Excuse me," and goes into the bathroom.

She closes the door and picks up her toothbrush. Just then the toilet bowl catches her eye. It's unnaturally white. The porcelain sparkles.

The sink and the bathtub and the floor tiles are shiny. There isn't a fleck of dirt anywhere. It takes her half an hour, at most, to make a bathroom this clean.

The bathroom is suddenly awash with possibility. Never before has she felt so fully in command of herself.

She locks the door, walks over to the tub, and sits down to savor the moment.

THE FULL RIDE

I could not have told you why I played football, but it wasn't for the physical contact. I never aimed at a running back's knee or speared a quarterback with my headgear, and instead of hammering offensive linemen with my forearm, I picked a gap and shot it. My coach said I played "soft" defensive tackle, the word "soft" sounding hard in his mouth. I ran a 4.8 forty, though, so the ball and I usually converged.

In 1976, my senior year, I visited State and Ole Miss and Southern and even Tennessee, but I'm just 6'1", short for a lineman, and none of the big schools signed me. Just when I thought I might not get a scholarship at all, Coach McGrath from Delta State drove down to Indianola and offered me what he called "the full ride." We agreed to sign the papers the next day.

Outside, in the parking lot, cold wind whipped my muffler. Putting on my gloves, I saw Mrs. Brunson, my English teacher, leave the building by the end door. I waved at her and started walking toward her green LTD. She had an armload of papers, so I tried to open the car door, but it was locked.

"Hold these," she said. She wore a white wool cap. Her cheeks were already red from the cold. I took the papers. While she fished in her purse for the car keys, I said, "I just got a scholarship."

"That's wonderful. Where?"

"Delta State."

She opened the car door. I handed her the papers, which she laid on the front seat. Then she turned and put her hands on my shoulders and standing on her toes kissed my cheek. "I'm proud of you," she said. "Are you happy?"

"Sure." My cheek felt warm where she'd kissed me.

"I'll be taking night courses up there next year," she said. "For recertification. I'll probably see you on campus."

She got into her car. I closed the door, and she backed out and drove away.

•   •   •

That spring my girlfriend broke up with me. I didn't want to see her with somebody else, so I skipped all the senior parties. Freed from football practice, I napped in the afternoon. At night I sat up late, reading Jack Higgins and Len Deighton and leaving every now and then to go outside and smuggle in beer—I'd stashed an ice chest in an empty tenant shack up the road from the house.

When I reported to Delta State, I was in terrible condition. I ran the opening mile in seven and a half minutes. Every day after wind sprints I threw up. Guys on the team, seeing me on campus, would grin and say, "Burrf." One day, when I was holding a blocking dummy during offensive line drills, Coach McGrath said, "Harper, move head-up on Bivens." I was standing there thinking that when we started live scrimmage, I might try to break my ankle—that would put me out for six weeks, and by then it would be October and cooler. I failed to move head-up on Bivens. Coach McGrath slapped my headgear. "Dumb ass. Move." I moved, but now I'd drawn his attention. "What'd you make on your ACT?"

I should've lied, but I didn't. "Thirty-one."

His jaw went slack. "Thirty-one?"

"Yes sir."

"What's your major?"

"English."

After that, I became the team joke. Somebody wrote on the door to my room, *Roses are red, violets are blue, I love to read, do you?* Somebody stuck a dead hawk in my bed. Somebody else dismantled my bed and toted it out to the parking lot, where they put it back together and parked it parallel. One night, when I was taking a shower, somebody turned out the bathroom light and started firing a pistol. Lying on the tiles, I could hear bullets knocking chunks from the wall.

I didn't play in the first game, which we lost 41–10. The following Tuesday we scrimmaged live from three until six. Lots of guys had blood on their jerseys. Several fights broke out. I was playing defensive tackle on the scout team, opposite Jim Buckner, who'd had a bad game against Murray State. Coach McGrath kept yelling, "Buckner, you're dragging your ass." I hated to hear that. I patted Buckner on the rear and said, "Don't let it get to you."

"Fuck your teeth," he said.

Next play he threw a forearm into my Adam's apple. He started hitting me late, punching me in the belly after the whistle blew. On a sweep the other way, he slammed into me, clenched my jersey in his fists, and drove me all the way to the sideline.

I said, "Easy, Buck."

He grabbed my face mask and twisted. Sweat droplets glistened in his moustache. "You shitass," he hissed. "This is serious."

Coach McGrath hollered, "Knock it off, Buckner. Harper don't want to play. His ass won't be here next year."

That evening, to avoid the athletic cafeteria, I drove out to the Pizza Hut and ordered a sandwich. When I turned away from the counter, someone called my name.

It was Mrs. Brunson. She was sitting in one of the booths. I walked over, and she said, "How's football?"

"It's not going too well."

"Is anybody with you?"

"No ma'am."

"Sit down then—I'm waiting on a pizza."

She was in her early thirties then, an attractive dark-haired woman who looked tan the year round. I made only a B− in her class—I neglected some of the assignments—but she always acted as if I were one of the top students.

"Tell me," she said. "What's going wrong?"

"Coach McGrath's stupid and mean. The guys on the team all major in either PE or criminal justice—they want to be guards at Parchman. They're sorry the Vietnam War ended." I stared at the red tablecloth. "I reported out of shape. I don't want to play anymore, but if I quit I lose my scholarship. My grades aren't good enough for an academic grant."

"I was afraid you'd have trouble playing college ball. Noel said you would."

Noel was her husband. I used to see him eating breakfast at Kelly's Truckstop, his face partially hidden by the *Delta Farm Bulletin*. He always wore khaki pants and workshirt, and in his hip pocket he carried a black New Testament.

I said, "I didn't know Noel played college ball."

"He didn't."

"So how could he be so sure I'd have problems?"

She stirred her Coke. "Noel has opinions about most things."

Soon the waitress brought our food. While we ate, Mrs. Brunson asked me how my classes were going.

"I've slept through most of them," I admitted.

"So why are you in college?"

"I'm doing research."

"On what?"

"Apes. I'm living among them."

"Oh, Lee." She giggled. When she did that, her whole face got into the act.

She asked me what I'd been reading.

"Adventure novels. Spy stuff."

She said, "That's to be expected." When I was in her class, she used to tell me that some popular fiction was okay, but she said I ought to read good books too. She claimed that would teach me discernment. Now she said, "If I loan you a good book, will you read it?"

"Sure."

From her purse she pulled *The Great Gatsby.* I had tried to read it in tenth grade but I lost interest when no one got killed by page 5. Still I accepted it from her. I didn't want to hurt her feelings.

"I'm teaching it later this year," she said, "so you'll have to give it back before long. I'll be up here every Tuesday evening." She said her mother-in-law picked her daughter up on Tuesdays so that she could drive to Delta State in the afternoon and spend some time in the library before class.

When she stood to leave, I noticed that she was wearing Levi's. This was the first time I'd seen her without a skirt on. She looked shapely in jeans.

•   •   •

We lost our next game 21–0. Afterwards McGrath said he intended to get rid of most of us before next year. He said we were just hanging around, consuming food and using too much tape on our ankles.

Tuesday, when practice ended, I took a fast shower, picked up *The Great Gatsby,* and jogged across campus to the library. There I roamed the stacks, searching for her, but I didn't see her. On my way to the athletic cafeteria, I glanced into the main dining hall, and there she was, sitting at a table in the corner, flipping through a poetry anthology.

She looked pleased to see me. "Sit down," she said. She pushed her tray of dirty dishes toward the edge of the table. I sat down and handed her *The Great Gatsby*.

"Did you like it?"

"It's better than *The Eagle Has Landed*."

"You don't say."

"I did like it."

"I'm glad," she said. "I think that as you get older, you'll appreciate great books more and more. You're too bright not to."

We sat there and talked for almost an hour. She told me she hoped I'd get serious about school. Though I might not realize it now, the grades I made my freshman year would follow me around later on. "Sometimes," she said, looking out the window at the infirmary, "people make mistakes when they're eighteen or nineteen that they can never undo. It's a crucial time in your life."

The next Tuesday, when I entered the cafeteria, she waved and motioned me over. "You won't believe what I just read," I said. "*Pride and Prejudice*. And nobody made me."

She laughed. "You're getting educated."

Once a week, for the next month and a half, I met her in the dining hall. The first couple of times, I was careful not to try and arrange our next encounter. I never said, "See you next Tuesday," because I thought that if I did, she'd frown like she used to in class when somebody gave a stupid answer. But after a while, I decided she looked forward to our meetings too.

She suggested I read *The Power and the Glory*. From the first page the book gripped me like nothing I'd ever read before. I plowed straight through it in a single day, skipping all my classes, pausing only to attend practice, at which I felt myself persecuted much like Father Montez. When I told Mrs. Brunson how much I liked the book, she frowned.

"Is something wrong?"

"Oh, no." She smiled and patted my hand. "I was just remembering a time when I asked somebody else to read that book."

"This other person didn't like it?"

"No," she said. "He couldn't understand why Greene wanted him to care about a priest who drank too much."

Sitting across the table from her, I began to notice things that had escaped my attention before. The way she wrinkled her nose when she smiled. The brown birthmark nestled in the cleft of her neck. At night, lying in bed, I imagined myself alone with her. I wondered what her hair would feel like. It looked soft, but I knew that only when you touched another's hair could you know its true texture.

•   •   •

The Tuesday before our last game, McGrath made us scrimmage until six-thirty. I reached the cafeteria at five till seven, and though I expected her to be gone, I found her sitting in our usual corner. A package wrapped in green paper lay on the table.

"Happy birthday," she said.

Last week I had told her that I would turn nineteen today. I tore off the paper and pulled out a hardcover copy of *Humboldt's Gift*.

I said, "Will you celebrate with me?"

"How?"

"We could go have a drink."

"I hardly ever drink." She glanced at her watch. "I've missed my class. Look, if you want to, maybe we could just take a short walk and I'd go home."

"We could drive over to the river."

She said, "Okay. But you'll have to bring me back in an hour."

We picked up my car and headed west on Highway 6. On the

way she told me she'd grown up in Rosedale. She said, "The levee was in our backyard." I asked if her parents still lived there, but she said they were both dead.

We crossed the levee on a gravel road that forked on the other side. She told me to go left. We drove through forest for a mile and emerged on a bluff above the river. She said, "Let's walk down to the water," so we left the car and stumbled down the hill.

Moonlight speckled the river. On the Arkansas side, there was nothing but a black wall of woods.

She said, "We used to come here in high school."

"Parking?"

"Yes. We did that even back then."

"It wasn't that long ago."

"It was very long ago."

We stood there looking out at the water. You could hear the current rushing in the channel. She said, "The river's so powerful."

"I went down on it skiing once," I said. "The current's scary."

"Noel swam across it when he was twenty. A mile or so below the Greenville bridge. The only reckless thing he ever did."

I said, "Were you very young when you married Noel?"

"I was the same age you are."

"I feel like I'd like to get married someday."

"Don't make a mistake."

"You mean don't get married?"

"I mean don't marry the wrong person."

She sat down on the ground and clasped her hands behind her knees. I sat cross-legged beside her. On the river, to the south, a string of lights appeared. Probably a barge.

After a while she said, "Lee, how do you feel about me?"

"Don't you know?"

"I don't know if I do or not."

My knees were shaking. I put my hands on them to steady them, but my hands started shaking too. I said, "I just wish you weren't married."

She closed her eyes and mouthed a word. It looked like "God."

I said, "I wouldn't have told you, but you asked."

She said, "Let's go back." She stood and climbed the hill.

I followed her to the car. When I got in, she said, "This is my fault. I should've stopped these weekly meetings."

She said it as if I were some stray hound she'd fed against her better judgment. I said, "So why didn't you, damn it?"

"Because I like to be with you."

When I put my arm around her, she stiffened. I drew her toward me. I would've let go if she'd resisted, but she didn't. I lifted her chin and pressed my mouth against hers.

We kissed a long time. Then she pulled away and began un-buttoning her blouse.

•   •   •

On the way back to town, she sat all the way across the seat, slumped against the door. She said nothing. Neither did I. I kept replaying that instant when she struggled out of her jeans and her flesh emerged pale grey in the dark.

I turned into the commuter parking lot and pulled up beside her car. She said, "I can't see you again."

"Why?"

"You know why."

"Please. Mrs.—"

"Jesus—use my first name."

"Jane. Please."

"No."

I reached for her. She grazed my cheek with her palm. Then she opened the door and jumped out.

The following night I drove to Indianola and parked behind the elementary school. From the playground I could see her house. I watched Noel sand a bookcase in the carport. Once she came out. They gestured, conferred. I squinted, searching their faces for some sign of disturbance, but I detected none. Noel laughed and picked up a paint can. She disappeared into the house.

I cut all my classes for the rest of the week. Lying in bed behind closed blinds, I remembered the taste of her mouth, the faint rose odor of her skin, the way she raked my shoulders with her nails. I was lying there Friday afternoon when the phone rang.

The operator said, "Hold, please." Someone fed a pay phone coins. "Go ahead."

"Lee?"

"Yes."

"It's me. I'll see you next week. If you still want to."

I said, "I do."

Football season was over, so we began meeting in the afternoons. I learned all the back roads, scouting the terrain in advance. My favorite was a turnrow near Shaw. The field it encircled lay fallow, and the road itself ended in a thicket two miles from the nearest house. We were there one Tuesday in December when she said, "Sooner or later this has to stop."

"Is Noel suspicious?"

"Of course not—he has too much else on his mind. The farm. His Sunday-school class."

"I can't understand how you ended up with him."

She shrugged. "Just did."

"Mistakes can be corrected."

She laid both palms on my face. "You have more options than I do," she said. "I have a little girl. Did you forget that?"

I had not forgotten it. I thought about it all the time. If she had no daughter, she could leave Noel and live with me. Where we would live, how we would live, I never considered.

I said, "I don't want it to stop."

"You think I do?"

"So we have to make some plans."

She pulled me toward her and hugged me. The strength with which she did it surprised me. I couldn't have wriggled loose if I wanted.

She said, "Don't ruin it."

•   •   •

That winter was one of the Delta's worst. Several nights the temperature dropped below ten degrees, a natural disaster down there. Snow became a common sight. The bad weather complicated matters. One week Noel made her miss class because freezing rain had iced the roads. Another time a snowstorm caught us in a cotton patch. I had to get behind the car and push while she floored the accelerator. The tires spattered me with black mud and snow.

She resisted talk of the future. Yet the future fueled my thinking. The only part of my week that mattered was the time I spent with her each Tuesday. When the spring semester ended and she had no more classes, there would be no excuse for her to drive to Cleveland. I could not imagine what I'd do then. Would I hang around the weight room with the guys on the team? To them, farting was the height of hilarity. Would I join a fraternity? Meet some nice girl in Algebra I and take her out to see *Star Wars?*

I developed insomnia. Late at night, I tried to read, but that proved impossible. I'd reach the end of a chapter, then realize I had no idea what the last twenty pages said. After a while, I gave up and turned to the TV, watching old serials on the all-night Memphis channel. Today, if I flip on the TV and see Jim Nabors or Buddy Ebsen or any of the other actors from the shows I watched then, a quiver runs through my stomach.

I lost my appetite and with it much weight. One day, on the sidewalk in front of Kethly Hall, I met Coach McGrath. He looked me up and down. "You're looking lean, Harper," he said. "You may play some ball after all."

I said, "Yes, sir," and walked on. I knew I would never play ball. I'd outgrown all games of that sort.

•   •   •

In April, spring training began. Practice lasted till five, and by the time I showered and dressed, it was usually five-thirty. On Tuesdays I left the dressing room running.

Since the weather was warm, she waited for me in her car, which she always parked in the same corner of the commuter parking lot. One evening I jogged up to the LTD, opened the door on the passenger side, and saw that she was reading *Little Dorrit,* with a pink EZ marker in her hand. She said, "Just a minute, honey," and went on reading.

That made me mad—so little time remained. School would end in three weeks. "Come on," I said, "it's the fourth quarter for us."

She looked up from the book. "Is that supposed to be funny?"

"Sports metaphor comes easy to a jock."

"I don't think of you as a jock. Do you want me to?"

I almost said, *No ma'am.* "No."

"All right." She finished reading and marking a page.

Our last time together she brought me another present, *The Riverside Shakespeare.* When I tore off the wrappings, we were sitting in her car on the bluff above the river, the same place we'd parked that night six months ago. It was daylight now. The sun turned the muddy water silver.

"That's a special present," she said. "Because you've been very special to me."

She wore her Levi's and a bright-red oversized jersey, and she looked a lot younger than thirty-two. Lately, what we were doing had ceased to bother her. She'd even suggested new ways to do it. Our couplings had begun to resemble the flexibility exercises McGrath made us do. The last two weeks, we'd made love outside, on a beach towel she'd bought for that purpose. The towel had a king-sized Eveready battery painted on it.

I said, "You're special to me too."

She slid across the seat, and I took her in my arms. "It's too bad," she said, "that we couldn't have been young at the same time. Wouldn't that have been nice?"

"Yes."

"You don't know what you've meant to me."

That was true. I did not know what I meant to her. I knew that I did not mean to her what she meant to me or we would not be so casually saying good-bye.

I said, "I don't know what I'll do now."

She said, "You'll be nineteen now. Enjoy it."

•   •   •

That night I paid one of the student trainers to steal me some codeine, and I took enough to knock myself out for about twelve hours. When I woke the next afternoon, I'd slept through two exams. The next day I missed two more. I'd cut so many classes and failed so many quizzes that I probably couldn't have passed my courses anyway, but the zeros on the exams removed all doubt. When grades came out the following week, I had an 0.0.

Coach McGrath phoned to say he'd have to revoke my scholarship. He said, "I'm sorry, Harper," and he told me again that he thought I could've played.

I was staying at my parents' house then. That afternoon I drove into Indianola. I passed Jane's house ten or twelve times before I finally drove by and found her car gone. That was what I'd been waiting for. I drove to Piggly Wiggly and, sure enough, there was her car. I parked several spaces away and walked into the store. She'd probably have her daughter with her, but I still hoped we might talk. I'd promised not to call or try to see her, so in an effort to make this look like chance, I grabbed a big jar of

Blue Plate mayonnaise from a floor display and threw it into a hand basket.

I found her in the pet-food aisle. Her daughter was with her and so was Noel. When she saw me, she froze. Then a smile popped out on her face, and she said, "Well, hi, Lee. How was your school year?"

She was smiling at me, and Noel was grinning and saying, "Hey, big fella," and reaching out to shake my hand.

I said, "My school year was great. Right up to the end." Then I shook hands with Noel and headed for the front of the store. I left the mayonnaise in a bin of M & Ms.

After supper that night, I told my mother and father that I'd flunked out of school and lost my scholarship. They were surprised and hurt, and they wanted to know what had happened. I blamed it on football. When my mother went to bed, my father sat up with me, asking questions, probing, and I finally admitted I'd had an affair with a much older woman. He tried to make me say who, but I refused because he's an explosive person sometimes and I was scared he'd shoot her or, if not that, at least tell the principal and make her lose her job.

My parents mortgaged their house and borrowed money to send me to Ole Miss—somehow, they got the school to admit me as a provisional student. For one-twenty a month, I lived in a room at Nelson's Motel. In the mornings I attended my classes, then I ate a quick lunch and went to the library, where I stayed until late at night. I studied so intensely that I often forgot where I was. When I took Shakespeare, I read the ten plays that were assigned and the twenty-six that were not. I read eight books listed in the bibliography in the back of *The Riverside Shakespeare*. I read six volumes of Studies in Shakespeare.

Ole Miss had a classics department, so I minored in Greek. I was the only minor that department ever had. The head, Dr. Betts, became friendly with me and invited me to his house a few times, though I annoyed him my senior year when I registered for Classical Studies 502: Directed Readings in Thucydides, Lysias, and Xenophon. He said, "Lee, we have to list a certain number of courses in order to get funding. We really hadn't expected anyone to enroll in that one."

I said, "I'm aching to read *Anabasis.*"

When I think of those days, I remember old books, the quiet isolation of a library cubicle, the green shag carpet in my room at the motel. I do not remember individual students. Instead, I remember all of the students on campus. I recall them as a moving particolored mass. I see them streaming out of Bondurant Hall, walking across the parking lot toward the cafeteria. I see them loitering in the grove, their faces indistinct, some of them holding hands. I hear their voices raised in unison at pep rallies on the square, and I hear late-night shouts and shrieks as they emerge in groups from The Gin. I watch them walk in twos and threes up University Avenue. They gesture toward one another. Their lips are moving, but I can only imagine what they say.

SOME GLAD MORNING

MOODY," he heard Rae holler. "Tim's waiting."

He balanced the guitar case on the arms of the chair, yelled, "Bye," to Rae in the kitchen, and wheeled himself out.

Tim hoisted the guitar into the back of the pickup, then helped Moody into the cab; he folded the wheelchair and stowed it with the guitar.

Cranking the truck, he said, "Got any new tunes?"

"Been working on a couple."

"About what?"

"Extinguishment of dreams."

"How come you don't write something positive?"

Moody shot a long look at Tim: his jaw was full of Red Man, his thinning hair half hidden by a NAPA parts cap.

"What do you mean," Moody said, "by *something positive?*"

"I just mean these songs you write, they're funny and all that and everybody gets a kick out of 'em, but what about you?"

"What about me?"

"I just been wondering if maybe they don't harm your self-image."

"You been going to the junior college?"

"Why the hell you ask me that?"

"'Self-image' sounds abnormal on your lips. I figured you heard it said elsewhere, and the junior college is the likeliest place."

Tim stayed quiet for two or three blocks. Finally he said, "What about your new neighbor?"

"What new neighbor?"

"Joe Pritchard's nephew. Just got his ass out of Parchman. I heard he was in for armed robbery. He's moved in with Mr. Pritchard and gone to work at his station fixing flats."

"Better remove the keys from my wheelchair at night."

Tim giggled. Moody felt relieved. Making somebody laugh at his own expense never failed to make him feel lighter. But it was a talent he could seldom command anymore. Unless he was singing. He knew he could count on it then.

The sign on the boat trailer at the Beer Smith Lounge said, *Tues–Sat Moody Bystrom.* There were ten or twelve pickups and a couple of cars in the parking lot.

The bar was a windowless room with a concrete floor, bare light bulbs dangling from the ceiling. Oak tables claimed the space in front of the stage. A shuffleboard stood far back by the door.

Tonight Moody wasted no time. He thumped the mike once and strummed a G chord to make sure the guitar was in tune. Somebody hollered, "Sing about hurt."

"I aim to," Moody said. "I've peed in the bushes with everybody here, so we'll dispense with the intro. Just get serious about your drinking and I'll sing a few tunes, mostly about loss and whatnot. Feel free to weep in your Millers."

He started off with a fast one—"On and On"—and came right back with "My Darlin' Corey Is Gone." The sound of his voice, detached and cool, not the least bit whiny, soothed his soul. He liked himself when he was singing.

Two more old ones, then: "Here's one of mine—wrote it just this morning. It's called 'The Last Time I Cared,' and here's how it goes."

Last time I cared a bit
Dick Nixon had just quit
And Gerald Ford was having
His brief day.
Aw, but that was such a long old time ago.
What I've come to I don't rightly know.
But it's a fate a truckload shares.
They mass-produce these chairs.
Gerald Ford was in the White House
The last time that I cared.

He sailed right through the stomping and the laughing into "I Got the Turnrow Blues."

•   •   •

When he got home, it was almost midnight. In his music room he took the guitar out of its case and began rubbing Fiddle Brite into what remained of the finish. The guitar was an old Martin; it had an inch-long gash in the top near the bridge, action half an inch high. He'd owned it since he was nine years old, and it was still the only instrument he ever played, even though Rae's daddy had given him a new D-45 last Christmas. He buffed the back and sides, wiped off the strings, and laid the guitar back in its case.

Rae lay on her belly, watching the Giants play the Braves. As soon as he rolled through the door, Moody smelled dope in the air.

"How'd it go?" she said.

"Pretty good. They put twenty-eight dollars in the box."

She pushed herself up on her arms. "That's really good, honey," she said. "And on a Tuesday night." She yawned. "I'm so tired," she said. "I wish I had tomorrow off."

Moody wanted to cry, and it was maddening not to know why. Nothing had changed in the last ten minutes. Nothing had changed in ten years. "If you want tomorrow off," he said, "why don't you just call your daddy and tell him? Tell him to send over a pair of good steaks and a bottle of Chivas. And a cook to fix the steaks—don't forget that."

"I'm sorry," she said. "I didn't mean it that way. I just meant I'd like to hang around home. With you."

He hated it when she felt sorry for him. "You've been smoking dope," he accused.

"Just a drag or two, Moody."

"I asked you not to."

"Honey, it eases my mind and helps me sleep."

"What's on your mind that makes it need easing?"

"Oh, *nothing*," she said. "Nothing's on my mind. Some people like to have a beer and unwind. I just like a joint sometimes."

Moody gripped the wheels and spun toward the door. "So go on," he said. "Go on and be easy."

•   •   •

Wednesday morning, while Rae was working the check-out stand, a guy she'd never seen before put a carton of Winstons on the counter. She said, "How are you?" and punched the register.

He said, "Fine. I think we might be neighbors."

He was short and thin, and he wore a pair of glasses with black plastic rims. A patch above the pocket on his workshirt said *Ed*. The workshirt looked strange on him. She had the impression he belonged behind a desk.

"Neighbors?" she said.

"I just moved in with Joe Pritchard. He's my uncle. I saw you out working in your garden yesterday. My name's Ed Poindexter."

"Mine's Rae. Rae Bystrom." She glanced at the register. "You owe Piggly Wiggly eight dollars and four cents."

"I owe some other people a lot more than that." He handed her a five and four ones.

She made change. "We didn't go to school together, did we?" she asked.

"College?"

"No, I mean high school."

"I'm not from Indianola. I went to high school in Biloxi."

"Why would anyone leave the Gulf Coast for the Delta?"

"It's a complicated story," he said. "What's the most exciting thing to do in Indianola at night?"

"Go to sleep."

"Is it that bad?"

A black woman rolled her cart into the check-out. "It depends on who you ask," Rae said. "You want a bag?"

"That's okay," he said.

She'd invited her father over to eat that evening, something she felt obliged to do at least once a month. He showed up wearing shorts and a tee shirt, hale after jogging five miles. At supper he tried to discuss the Ole Miss football team with Moody. "I don't know about Brewer," he said. "You know he's going to the I this fall? If he had a real fullback, somebody like you, that might work. But with those fast little backs he's got now, he's better off in an option offense."

Rae said, "I met this guy named Ed today. He just moved in with Mr. Pritchard. His nephew. I didn't get to talk to him long enough to find out what he's doing here."

Moody said, "He just got out of Parchman."

"I don't believe it!"

Moody's fork halted. A broccoli spear dangled, dripping butter. "Why don't you believe it?" he asked. The broccoli spear disappeared into his mouth.

"He just didn't look like the type. It must've been a white-collar crime."

"I guess you could perform armed robbery in a white collar."

"Armed robbery," her father whistled.

"Who told you that?" she said.

"Tim."

"Consider your source."

"I'm just telling you what I heard."

"Okay," she said. "Maybe it's true. But he was just kind of small and polite and—hell, I don't know."

"It's those little son of a bitches you have to watch," her father said. "A big guy like me or like—"

Oh, Daddy, she thought. Please.

He caught himself too late. The word "Moody" fizzled, died.

She felt sorry for him when he looked down at his plate. "Moody," he said, "I'm an asshole."

"That's all right, Walter," Moody said. "You do have to watch the little son of a bitches. The big ones too."

•   •   •

Her father said he needed to leave early and check on his catfish ponds, but she knew he was just embarrassed. He'd never gotten used to seeing Moody in a wheelchair. It had been over ten years since Moody played football, yet her father still thought of him as a fullback.

She cleared the table, washed the dishes. She heard floorboards creaking, Moody moving through the house. Tonight, while he was eating, she'd noticed again how flaccid his jaws were. Same as his chest and arms. And his legs were so thin. They belonged on a hen.

There was a time when his body had scared her. Several months after the accident, she found a pressure sore on his hip. Numb from the waist down, he lay on his right side night after night, without rolling over, until a hunk of flesh collapsed. She saw it when she was giving him a bath. She put her hands in her hair and screamed. Moody gazed down at the open sore, wide as a quarter and half an inch deep. He reached his arm around her and said, "Don't cry, honey. Just call the service station." She blubbered, "Why?" and he said, "Tell 'em you've got a flat that needs patching."

She dried the dishes and went into his room. He sat there changing his strings. "Did you intend to drive yourself in tonight?"

He pushed in a bridge pin. "Beer said he'd come get me."

"I was thinking I might come listen a while." She would have gone every night if she wasn't always so tired. She liked him when he was sitting up there singing. "Okay if I call Beer and tell him I'll bring you?"

When he looked at her, she could see he wasn't mad anymore. His anger cooled as fast as it boiled. "Sure," he said. "Any requests?"

"How about 'Summer Wages.'"

"I'll do it."

There were eight or nine guys in the lounge. She waved at Tim and Ricky Voss. While Moody tuned up, she sat on a barstool. Beer Smith ambled over, and she said, "Draw me a Bud Light."

He brought it, glanced at Moody. "I heard from the guy at MCA," he said.

This was one of the reasons she'd come. "So?"

"He said Moody's playing and singing are too bluegrassy and his original songs are too personal and weird. I guess it's a good thing we sent the tape without telling him."

"I guess so."

Beer drummed thick fingers on the bar. "You doing okay yourself?"

"Just fine."

"You look a little tired."

"Probably just old age."

"You're still a young woman."

He'd driven her and Moody's school bus when they were kids, and his hair had been white even then. When he asked Moody to sing here, he hadn't known it'd pay off.

"I'm fine," she said.

Up on the stage Moody was ready. He'd decided to lay some gospel on them. "Ricky Voss," he called. "Brother Voss, are you saved?"

"Hell, I don't hardly know, Moody. I been baptized, but seem like lately the spirit ain't in me."

"I believe," Moody whispered, "Brother Voss wants reviving."

He flatpicked a melody he'd loved all his life, then he closed his eyes and sang "Will the Circle Be Unbroken." They joined him on every chorus. He segued into "I Saw the Light." Then he sang another one he loved, the one that held a promise, the only truth he felt in useless limbs and shattered spine.

> Some glad morning
> When this life is o'er
> I'll fly away.
> To a home
> On God's celestial shore.
> I'll fly away.

On her barstool Rae had quit singing. She knew how much Moody meant those words.

•   •   •

The next evening, after Moody left for the bar, she decided to mow the lawn. She went out back and poured gas into the mower from the red can kept beneath the porch. Then she pushed the mower into the front yard and started wrestling the starter.

"Need a hand?"

She turned and saw Ed standing on his uncle's porch. "I think I need about three more hands than I've got," she said. "I have a hell of a time starting this thing."

He walked across the street. "What's that extra set of handles for?"

"That's a deadman device. You have to squeeze both handles at the same time you pull the starter. If you let go of the handles, the mower goes dead."

He grabbed the handles and jerked the cord. The motor came loudly to life.

"Thanks," she hollered.

He yelled back, "I'll mow for a beer."

"Are you serious?"

"My uncle's a Baptist. No drinking in his house."

"You've got a deal."

He finished about eight. She had two beers standing on the coffee table when he knocked. He sat down beside her on the couch and took a long swallow. He said, "I never liked beer very much until I was where I couldn't have it. Then I craved it all the time."

"How long were you in jail?"

He laughed. "Who says I was in jail?"

"News is contagious in this place."

"I served a year."

"Then you couldn't have done what I heard."

"What'd you hear?"

"Armed robbery."

"I *was* armed," he said. "With a checkbook. My wife was the most frugal person in the world until she met me. I was sentenced to eighteen months for kiting." He shook his head. "Whenever I found something I wanted, I couldn't be calm till I'd bought it. Even if I had no money."

"You seem calm now."

"Serving time," he said, "can force a calmness on you."

She guessed that might be true. As long as you knew when your sentence was up. She said, "What happened to your wife?"

"She's divorcing me."

They drank their beers slowly. He told her he'd taught American history at Gulfport High School but getting another teaching job, at least in Mississippi, would be impossible. He said he'd probably leave the state when he could afford it.

"So you were a teacher," she said. "I didn't go to college."

"It's expensive now."

"That wasn't why I didn't go."

"I know. Your father's the catfish king."

"Who says so?"

"Uncle Joe. He also says your husband's the most popular man in town and a real good musician."

"He has a big local following. Did Mr. Pritchard tell you why he's in the wheelchair?"

"Construction accident?"

"Two months after we got married and two weeks before we were supposed to start school at Ole Miss. He was working with his father on a house. A support collapsed. He had a football scholarship, too."

"Ole Miss wouldn't honor it?"

"No, they would've, but he was in the hospital for several months, and then for almost a year after he got out, he needed me with him most of the time. He had to relearn everything. And we had so many bills after all that that I just had to go to work. My father could've helped us, but of course we wanted to make it on our own. Looking back, I'm not so sure we made the smartest choice."

"My uncle said he's heard your husband's songs are real funny. In Parchman, the guys who did best were the ones who managed to keep a sense of humor. You must have a lot of courage," he said.

"Me?"

"You've stood by him."

She drained the last of her beer. "Standing by him's not so hard as you make it sound," she said.

He looked as if he were about to apologize, but apparently he thought better of it. They talked about the town some more; then he glanced at his watch and said he guessed he'd better go.

He came again a couple of nights later, bringing with him a six-pack of Moosehead. "I'll let you have three," he said, holding up the carton, "if you'll give me a place to drink."

They carried the beer onto the back porch and sat in her lawn chairs. "It's good," she said after a few swallows.

"Good and cold."

"Five twenty-eight a six-pack?"

"A little more at Mr. Quik."

A dark strip above his lip suggested plans for a moustache. Was he growing one?

"Thought I'd try it again," he said. "I had one before, but it was too sparse. I looked like I was twelve."

She said, "Do you ever smoke a joint?"

"I've been known to."

"Let's go inside," she said.

They sat on the floor in the living room and passed the joint. After a while she felt the tingle in her spine, the greyness creeping into her head. It turned into a nice numb high. She was surprised when he put his arm around her.

He exerted gentle pressure on her shoulders. She held back. Male smells teased her. He drew her to his chest, cupped a palm and ran it over her head.

He seemed to know where the bedroom would be. Salting her face with kisses, he led her down the hall.

"Not in the bedroom," she said. "In here."

In the guest room she let him pull her onto the sofa bed. Once there, she whispered, "We shouldn't."

He whispered "I know" and pulled off his shirt.

She let him undress her. When she felt him inside her, she said, "No. Don't move. Please."

"Why?"

"I'm afraid you'll make me pregnant."

He sighed and looked away. "Whenever a woman says no to me," he said, "I assume she means it. It usually turns out she didn't. We both end up thinking I'm a wimp."

"I don't think that."

He brightened. "Let's handle it this way. Don't say yes and don't say no. Just say what you'd like right now."

"You know what I'd like," she said.

•   •   •

When she was eighteen, she'd felt forty. Now she was twenty-eight, and for a few hours every evening, she felt eighteen.

Every evening, Tuesday through Saturday, she waited for Ed. He told the Pritchards he was going to a movie or to the poolroom, then he slipped into the alley behind her house and scaled the wooden fence. Usually he brought good beer, Beck's or Moosehead, which he'd hand down from his perch on the fence. Once, when he heard footsteps in the alley behind him, he tumbled headfirst into her yard.

"Oh God," she said. "Not again."

He sat up and rubbed his shoulder. "Moody hit concrete," he told her.

They drank two or three beers every evening. Then they went into the guest room and made love on the unfolded sofa bed. Ed's appetite for her was boyish.

"When you come," she told him, "you sound like Mr. Coffee."

He said he'd wanted to go to bed with her the first time he saw her. She said that didn't surprise her, considering where he'd been. Going to bed with him hadn't crossed her mind until after she did it. He asked her if she'd had many affairs, and she told him, "You're the second man I've slept with."

One night he lay holding her, stroking her hair. "What if I don't leave town?" he said.

"You have to leave," she said. "Go someplace and start over."

"What if I stayed? Would you keep seeing me?"

"There's no decent job for you here. You have no business fixing flats and pumping gas the rest of your life."

"You run a check-out stand."

"I have to."

"If I stayed, would you keep seeing me?"

"I guess I would."

"What if Moody found out?"

"We can't let that happen," she said.

A few nights later, she decided to talk. "About four years ago," she told him, "Moody started sinking into these really terrible depressions, going through periods where he'd barely talk at all for two or three days at a time. He didn't have the thing at Beer's then. He just had to sit around the house all day long by himself. And he started being suspicious of me. He thought I was doing what I'm doing now, which I wasn't.

"One day, Carl Reed, the guy who runs the Western Auto, came into the grocery store and mentioned that Moody had been in that morning and bought a handgun. I was so scared I kept calling home all day long, thinking up every excuse I could, just to make sure. I know that when he was buying the gun, he intended to use it."

"So," Ed said, "why didn't he?"

"Two reasons, I think. Right after he bought the gun was when Beer asked him to sing. That gave him something to feel good about."

When she didn't say anything else, Ed said, "What was the other reason?"

"I'm the other reason," she said. "And that's why we can't let him find out. Killing him would be kinder."

•   •   •

Suspicion, Moody had discovered, was a faithful sidekick. He could try to ignore it, he could talk down to it, Marshal Dilloning its Chester, yet there it was. Hopping along. And because it could hop, it kept overtaking him.

He went into the guest room looking for an old pair of khakis he thought Rae might have hung in the closet. When he opened the closet door, something white caught his eye. It was a sheet, rolled into a ball and stuffed into the far corner. He started to lean in and pick it up, but something warned him not to. He turned his chair and gazed at the sofa bed.

For two days he managed to stay out of the room. He watched Rae closely, but her behavior wasn't unusual. Hoping to silence his suspicions, he went back.

The white sheet was gone, a green one in its place.

•   •   •

The proof eliminated all previous misgivings. Rae wouldn't have done it with anyone he knew; no one he knew would have done it with Rae. It had to be a stranger.

A few weeks ago, he'd heard that Pritchard's nephew had gone to jail not for armed robbery but for writing bad checks. He'd seen the guy once or twice, leaving for work early in the morning. The time Rae mentioned meeting him in the store, he'd suffered the fit of wariness a jealous husband always feels toward new male neighbors, but she'd never mentioned the guy again, and he'd forgotten.

That evening, during his break at Beer's, he phoned his house. There was no answer. He called Joe Pritchard's. When Joe answered, he disguised his voice and asked to speak to Ed.

Joe Pritchard said, "He went out."

"When's the best time to reach him?"

"Between about six-thirty and eight. He usually goes out after that. Can I ask who's calling?"

"An old jailmate of his," Moody said and hung up.

When he got home Rae asked, "Did you call tonight?"

"No," he said. "Why?"

"Oh, the phone rang while I was in the tub. By the time I got to it, no one was on."

He had no appetite the next morning, but he made himself eat. Between bites, he glanced at her. She wore the pink cotton blouse he'd bought her last Christmas; her hair, freshly washed, reflected sunlight from the window.

When she started out the front door, he said, "Bye, Rae."

She was fumbling with her keys. "Bye, honey," she said.

He'd lain awake all night thinking what to put in his note. He couldn't write the whole truth: part of the truth was that she had somebody else now and he couldn't live thinking she might come home one day and say she was going to leave him. He could write the rest of the truth—that living half a life, through no fault of hers, had been hell from the very beginning—but putting that into words proved impossible.

He gave up and phoned Beer Smith. "This is Moody," he said.

"Hey, how's it going?"

"Listen, I'm fixing to kill myself," he said. "What I want you to do is come over here and take care of things so Rae doesn't find me. I haven't told anybody this, but I've been having a lot of bad pain lately, and I'm just tired of it. Tell her I love her, Beer."

He hung up before Beer could say a word.

In his room he opened the bottom desk drawer and took out his .38. He clicked the safety off and stuck the barrel in his mouth.

The phone started ringing.

The metal lay cold on his tongue, the trigger teased his finger. He closed his eyes and squeezed.

Nothing happened.

His hands were shaking. When he could halfway control them, he released the cylinder. Every chamber was empty.

He'd cleaned it four or five months ago, and it had been loaded then. He slammed it down on the desktop and reopened the drawer.

The box of cartridges was gone. He ransacked every drawer in the desk but couldn't find the bullets. Rae must have taken them and hidden them somewhere.

•   •   •

He heard Beer Smith burning rubber at the corner. Beer braked, started to jump out, then saw him sitting on the porch.

He walked over to the steps and planted a scuffed boot on the bottom one. "What in the hell did you mean calling me like that?" he said. "You ain't dead."

"Did you call anybody?"

"I started to call the ambulance, but I figured if you actually aimed to kill yourself, you'd do a thorough job."

"I didn't actually aim to do it." He'd had no time to think of what to say; he hoped it sounded convincing. "I *have* been hurting a lot, though, and I don't know, for a second there this morning I'd just had enough. But I didn't want to do it. Forgive me, Beer."

"I've got a good mind not to."

"Come on."

"All right. Hell, I can't afford a tiff with you. If you quit singing for me, I'd lose all my customers."

"Don't tell Rae," Moody said.

When Beer left he went back into his room and laid the gun in the drawer exactly as it had been. She'd never know he'd touched it. He wheeled himself back onto the porch.

Fall had come and with it the garlicky reek of defoliant. He sat on the porch and watched the breeze rustling the branches. At the Compress the noon horn blared.

He knew he would never learn to like it. But he also knew that Rae didn't want to be rid of him. And if she could live with it, so could he.

She returned at six, carrying a Piggly Wiggly sack, and asked if his day had been okay.

He said he'd learned a new tune.

•   •   •

The day before Christmas, she and Ed exchanged presents in her parked car, on the back side of a cotton patch near Cleveland. She gave him a nice flannel shirt and, as a gag, a moustache to glue on because his hadn't grown. He gave her a string of pearls. She held the necklace in her hand. The hopelessness of their situation struck home, but before she could say anything, he said, "You'll wear it when you're with me," so she nodded and put the necklace on.

One night in the middle of January he came over to the house, and she knew he had something to tell her.

"What is it?" she said.

"I got offered a teaching job."

"Where?"

"A reform school. In Christiansburg, Virginia. I know the guy who runs it."

She opened two of the beers he'd brought. "You'll be able to do some good at a reform school," she said.

"I don't know what to do."

"You'll go to Virginia."

"I don't want to leave you."

She handed him one of the beers. "I know. But there isn't a

damn thing we can do." She sat down at the kitchen table and rested her chin in her hands. She felt like he was already gone. "You'll go," she said.

"You wouldn't come with me?"

"I can't."

"What if I don't go?"

He wanted her to make his decision. "If you stay here past the time school starts, I'll stop seeing you," she lied.

"Will you see me until then?"

They both knew the question was absurd. He came around behind her and laid his hands on her shoulders. She raised her beer and took a bitter swallow.

When he left in late August, he asked her to rent a post office box so he could write to her, but she said no. She said good-bye to him at the airport in Greenville. After the plane took off, she walked into the bathroom, sat down in a stall, and cried. Only when she opened the door did she notice the row of urinals against the wall.

•   •   •

It was three weeks later when the change in Moody's behavior registered. He called her one night from Beer's. She was sitting on the couch, staring out the window at Joe Pritchard's house.

"I'm on break," Moody said. "How's it going?"

"Okay."

"You haven't heard about the Indians, have you?"

"What Indians?"

"These were real Indians. From India. Ricky Voss said somebody called the police station today and said there were three folks, dressed all in white, lying in the middle of 82, right in front of the Skate-a-Rama. Chief Towns told Ricky and Buster Morrison to go see what was happening.

"They drove out there, and sure enough, these Indians were just lying there with their eyes closed. They were even wearing turbans. Buster said, 'Who the hell are y'all?' but they didn't say a word. So he asked them, 'Well, where was y'all headed?' One of them opened his eyes and said, 'Nirvana.'

"So poor old Buster turned to Voss and said, 'Nirvana? Ain't that up close to Tutwiler?'"

Her laughter sounded good. They talked a few minutes more, then he said he had to play another set but he'd be home fairly early if she wanted to wait up.

She hung the phone up, still smiling at Buster's remark. Then something occurred to her. Moody was phoning her every night. He also called her during the day, when she was at work. He was cracking jokes, picking and singing for her when he came home from Beer's, laughing like he hadn't laughed in years.

She tried to remember when this started. It seemed to her that it had been going on for just about three weeks.

When he returned at eleven, she said, "Sing me a song."

"Which one?"

"One of your own."